# A VERY MERRY KRAMPUS CHRISTMAS

*Patti Petrone Miller*

Patti Petrone Miller

Copyright © Patti Petrone Miller 2024

No part of this publication may be reproduced, stored in a retrieval system, or transmitted, in any form or by any means, without the prior permission in writing of the publisher, nor be otherwise circulated in any form of binding or cover other than that in which it is published and without a similar condition including this condition being imposed on the subsequent purchaser.
FBI Anti-Piracy Warning: The unauthorized reproduction or distribution of a copyrighted work is illegal.
Criminal copyright infringement, including infringement without monetary gain, is investigated by the FBI and is punishable by up to five years in federal prison and a fine of $250,000.
A Very Merry Krampus Christmas First Edition Copyright © November 2024 by Patti Petrone Miller

Cover art by TMT Book Cover Designs
Published by AP Miller Productions All rights reserved.
Your support of the author's rights is appreciated.

# A Very Krampus Christmas

For my Best Girl in the Whole Wide World Tessa Wessa my Beenie Weenie

December 28 2006 - November 20 2023

Patti Petrone Miller

## Authors Book List

Accidental Vows
A Very Merry Krampus Christmas
Sin Takes A Holiday
Barking Up The Wrong Bakery, Thankgiving
Barking Up The Wrong Bakery, Christmas
Best Served Dead
Bewitching Charms
Christmas at Hollybrook Inn
Christmas on Peppermit Lane
Cabinet of Curiosities
Krampus
Hex and the City
Love in Stitches
Pies and Perps
Spectres and Souffles
Mamma Mia It's Murder
Once Upon A Christmas
The Fatman
The Frosted Felony
The Purr-fect Suspect
The Boogeyman
The Gingerdead Men
Vikings Enchantress
Welcome to Scarecrow Hollow
The Pendleton Witches
The Cabinet of Curiosities
Christmas In Pine Haven
Love in the Stacks
Once Upon A Christmas
Frosted Felony

# A Very Krampus Christmas

# Chapter 1

Merry awoke to the distant laughter of her nieces and nephews echoing up from downstairs, their excitement unmistakable. She stretched, savoring the warmth beside her as Christmas morning dawned over Tannenbaum Falls. She turned, meeting the familiar, joyful gaze of Klaus, who was already awake and smiling.

"Merry Christmas, my love," he murmured, his voice as soothing as hot cocoa on a winter's morning.

"Merry Christmas, Klaus," Merry replied, leaning closer. She took in his familiar scent—a mix of pine and cinnamon—and breathed deeply, feeling right at home.

Klaus chuckled, a warm, rich sound that reverberated through his chest. "I think I hear a few eager elves downstairs," he said, referring to the children waiting impatiently for the festivities to begin.

Merry grinned, nudging him. "I'm surprised they haven't stormed the room by now! Remember last year?"

"Ah, the infamous Christmas Morning Ambush," Klaus said with a laugh. "Who could forget?"

Giggling, Merry kissed his cheek before sliding out of bed. "We'd better head down before they break in. I can almost feel their excitement from here."

They rose and dressed, the ease and comfort between them warming Merry's heart. It felt natural to be here on Christmas morning, hand in hand, ready to greet their families and create new memories. She gave Klaus's hand a squeeze, reflecting on how lucky she felt to have him in her life. "This really is perfect," she said quietly.

Klaus's expression softened as he brought her hand to his lips. "No, Merry—you're what makes everything perfect."

As they stepped into the hallway, the sound of children's voices grew louder. Merry could hear her mother laughing and her father sharing stories with Klaus's family, filling the house with warmth. Hand in hand, she and Klaus headed downstairs, ready to embrace all the magic and mayhem Christmas day promised.

When they entered the kitchen, it was a festive whirlwind. The sunlight streamed through frosted windows, casting a glow over the snowy evergreens outside. Merry noticed two red aprons hanging on the pantry door, each embroidered with their names in shimmering gold.

"Oh, Klaus!" she exclaimed, tracing her fingers over the delicate stitching. "When did you make these?"

Klaus only smiled as he handed her one of the aprons. "A toymaker never reveals his secrets. Let's just say some elves may have helped."

They slipped into their matching aprons, and Merry couldn't help but giggle at the sight of Klaus—a centuries-old Christmas spirit—looking completely at ease in her cozy kitchen. She adjusted a stray lock of his hair with a smile.

"So, what shall we start with for our feast?" Klaus asked, glancing around the kitchen.

Merry considered their options. "We have to make Grandma's cinnamon rolls, of course. And your father mentioned something about an old recipe for spiced hot chocolate?"

The two of them moved around the kitchen in a familiar rhythm, gathering ingredients and preparing the oven. Merry watched as Klaus meticulously measured the flour, and her heart swelled with love and gratitude. This was her Christmas miracle, she realized—a holiday shared with him.

"You know," she said as she cracked eggs into a bowl, "if someone told me last Christmas that I'd be spending this one with a magical toymaker, I'd have thought they'd been at the eggnog."

Klaus chuckled as he stirred the ingredients. "And if someone had told me I'd find happiness in a small-town bakery, I'd have sent them straight to Krampus."

They laughed, reminiscing about how they'd met and all they'd been through together. "It's been quite a journey," Merry said, adding vanilla to the mix. "From that first moment you showed up in my grandmother's bakery to all the ways you've made this holiday special."

Klaus paused, looking at her with a gentle smile. "Merry, this journey has been a gift in itself. You've taught me more about the meaning of Christmas than I've learned in ages."

Merry felt a rush of love and hugged him tightly. "You're the real miracle, Klaus," she whispered.

As they prepared the rest of the breakfast, the room filled with the aroma of cinnamon and vanilla, setting a warm and joyful mood for the day. Soon, the platters were filled with golden waffles, crisp bacon, and a steaming pot of spiced cocoa.

At the table, Merry's family gathered, their faces bright with anticipation. "Breakfast is served!" Merry called, placing the tray of waffles in the center of the table.

Klaus set down the hot cocoa with a proud smile. "And what's Christmas without a touch of sweetness?"

Everyone dug in, laughter and chatter filling the room. Merry's mother leaned over, her expression conspiratorial. "So, Merry, dear... when can we expect little elves running around?"

Merry nearly choked on her waffle, her cheeks flushing. "Mom!"

Klaus smoothly interjected, ever the gentleman. "We're savoring each magical moment, aren't we, my love?" He squeezed her hand, and Merry's heart overflowed with gratitude.

When breakfast was finished, Merry stood up, clapping her hands. "Time for the next tradition!"

The children cheered as Klaus joined her, his voice warm and playful. "Lead the way, my Christmas cookie."

They guided the family to the living room, where gifts awaited beneath the Christmas tree. As the children tore through wrapping paper, the room filled with delighted gasps and heartfelt thank-yous. Klaus handled each gift he received with reverence, savoring even the simplest presents. When Merry handed him a hand-knitted scarf, he pulled her into a hug, murmuring, "It's perfect."

"It's to remind you of me whenever you're spreading Christmas cheer," she said softly.

"Every day reminds me of you," he replied. "You've brought Christmas to life for me."

Their families exchanged happy smiles as the couple shared a quick kiss, radiating warmth and love that filled the entire room.

With wrapping paper cleaned up and gifts enjoyed, Merry felt a renewed sense of gratitude. She clasped Klaus's hand as they approached the grand Christmas tree, its branches laden with lights and ornaments that held memories from years past. "Look at all these memories," she murmured, touching a glass snowflake her grandmother had given her.

"Yes," Klaus replied, admiring a wooden nutcracker he'd carved years ago, "each decoration a piece of us."

They joined hands, inviting everyone to share in a quiet moment of reflection. The joy, warmth, and love surrounding them felt like the truest Christmas magic, and Merry knew this was the perfect way to start the day.

"Who's ready to bake cookies?" she asked, her enthusiasm contagious.

A chorus of agreement followed as they made their way back to the kitchen. Klaus grinned as he put on the "Kiss the Cook" apron Merry had given him. Together, they gathered around the counter, pulling out her grandmother's recipe box.

"Alright, troops," Klaus said, taking charge with a grin. "Let's make some holiday magic!"

As they worked together, flour dusted the air like fresh-fallen snow. Merry laughed as she rolled out the dough, watching Klaus cut shapes with meticulous care. The kitchen filled with the sound of her mother's stories and the comforting aroma of baking cookies.

When the timer chimed, Merry pulled out the last batch of sugar cookies, admiring their perfect golden edges. Klaus reached for a cookie, only for Merry to playfully swat his hand away. "Not yet, Mr. Claus," she teased. "These are for the neighbors."

He chuckled, pulling her into a quick hug. "Old habits die hard."

They arranged the cooled cookies on platters, each one a small gift of Christmas cheer. Merry's mother handed them a stack of colorful tins. "For easier delivery," she said with a wink.

They packed up the tins and loaded them into their car, ready to spread a bit of Christmas magic throughout Tannenbaum Falls.

Their first stop was Mrs. Finklestein's cottage. The elderly woman welcomed them with a delighted smile, her face brightening when Merry presented a tin of cookies. "Merry Christmas, Mrs. Finklestein! We brought some treats just for you."

Mrs. Finklestein's voice trembled with emotion. "Oh, you're too kind. This is just what I needed."

Back in the car, Merry beamed at Klaus. "Did you see her joy? It's moments like these that make it all worthwhile."

Klaus nodded, sharing in her sense of purpose. "Indeed. It's these little acts that hold the true spirit of Christmas."

They continued making rounds, meeting friends and neighbors, each stop filling Merry's heart with a deeper sense of fulfillment. She couldn't help but notice the effect Klaus had on everyone they visited, his presence creating a warmth that lingered long after they left.

The day ended with the two of them returning home as the sky turned shades of pink and orange. Inside, they collapsed onto the couch, snuggling close as they reflected on a day filled with love, laughter, and community.

"What a perfect day," Merry murmured. She nestled closer, feeling a contentment she had never known. This was Christmas, she realized—a holiday she would cherish forever.

Klaus tightened his hold on her, his voice soft. "It truly was, my love."

As the Christmas lights glowed softly around them, they remained there in the quiet peace of each other's company, their love warming the room like the gentle crackle of a fireplace on a cold winter's night. Merry nestled against Klaus, her heart brimming with gratitude. She thought about how much her life had changed since she'd first come to Tannenbaum Falls. This town, with its snow-dusted streets and twinkling lights, had felt like a fresh start. But she never could have imagined how magical it would truly become.

"Klaus," she murmured, her voice barely above a whisper, "do you think... that all of this, what we've shared today with the town...do you think we've made a difference?"

Klaus turned, his expression gentle. "I know we have, Merry. Sometimes, it's not grand gestures but small, thoughtful moments that change people's hearts. A smile, a shared memory, a simple cookie. It's these things that fill Christmas with joy."

Merry felt the weight of his words, realizing how true they were. As she thought back to each stop they'd made, every happy face they'd seen, her heart swelled. "You're right. This day was more perfect than I could have ever hoped for."

They sat together in companionable silence, their thoughts drifting over the day's events. Soon, a gentle knock at the door startled them from their quiet reflection.

"Expecting someone?" Klaus asked, an eyebrow raised with intrigue.

Merry shook her head as she got up, crossing to the door and opening it to reveal her sister Sarah, holding her young son, Ethan, who clutched a small, wrapped gift.

"Merry! We had to stop by one last time," Sarah said, her cheeks rosy from the cold. "Ethan insisted on giving you this."

Merry knelt down to Ethan's height, smiling at the shy look on his face. "For me? Thank you, Ethan," she said, her voice warm. She unwrapped the small box to find a handcrafted ornament—a simple wooden star, painted in bright, cheerful colors.

"I made it for you, Aunt Merry," Ethan said, his voice barely above a whisper. "So you'll always remember Christmas here in Tannenbaum Falls."

Touched beyond words, Merry gathered Ethan into a warm hug. "It's perfect, thank you, sweetheart. I'll treasure it always."

After a few more exchanges of holiday well-wishes, Sarah and Ethan departed, leaving Merry and Klaus alone again. She hung the ornament on their tree, the little wooden star catching the light and casting a soft glow over the room.

Klaus stepped up beside her, slipping an arm around her shoulders. "This town loves you, Merry," he murmured, his voice low and sincere. "You've made Tannenbaum Falls feel like home for so many."

Merry felt a familiar warmth in her chest, a sense of belonging she hadn't known she was searching for. "It's funny," she said, leaning her head on Klaus's shoulder, "when I first came here, I thought it was just a job—a way to keep my grandmother's bakery alive. But now, I can't imagine being anywhere else."

Klaus tightened his hold on her, the two of them standing in quiet contemplation before the twinkling lights of the Christmas tree. "And I can't imagine being anywhere without you," he replied softly.

As the night wore on, they shared stories, laughter, and quiet moments by the fire, soaking in the magic of Christmas together. Merry realized that it was the simplest things—shared cookies, warm embraces, quiet moments—that created the memories she would carry with her always.

Finally, as the clock struck midnight, Merry and Klaus exchanged one last kiss, sealing a Christmas that had been filled with love, laughter, and community. Tannenbaum Falls, with its snow-covered streets and heartfelt traditions, had become a place where dreams came true and magic lived in every corner. And in Klaus's arms, Merry knew she had found her own little corner of Christmas magic.

In the glow of the Christmas lights and the warmth of their love, Merry felt a happiness that would carry her through every season to come. This was her Christmas miracle, wrapped up in a small-town bakery, a handful of cookies, and a heart that had found its true home.

## Chapter 2

The main street of Tannenbaum Falls glowed under layers of shimmering tinsel and radiant lights, transforming the town into a winter wonderland. Merry North stepped onto the snow-dusted sidewalk, her breath catching at the sight of the bustling activity as the town prepared for its annual Christmas festival. It was as if every corner, every storefront, and every lamppost held a bit of magic.

Colorful garlands looped between lampposts, and the scent of pine and cinnamon drifted through the crisp winter air. Merry pulled her red knit scarf tighter and adjusted her Santa hat, feeling a spark of excitement pulse through her. She glanced at the twinkling wreaths adorning the doors of the shops and imagined the festivities that lay ahead.

As Merry strolled down Main Street, she paused in front of Frosty's Sweets, where the window displayed an impressive gingerbread house village. Intricate sugar details decorated each cookie-sized home, complete with frosting icicles and tiny gumdrop pathways. Inspiration sparked as she imagined creating a similar display for her own bakery, filled with gingerbread men and houses for the children in town to admire.

"I can't believe the festival is almost here," came a voice from across the street. Merry turned and spotted two women chatting in front of the town's towering Christmas tree.

"I know! And they're still looking for volunteers," the other woman replied, her mittened hands waving for emphasis. "There's still so much to do. I hope it all comes together."

The conversation caught Merry's interest, and she found herself slowing to listen more closely. She wanted so much to help out with the festival—it was one of the town's most treasured traditions, after all. Her grandmother, Millie, had always been involved, and Merry couldn't help but feel it was her duty to step in and fill her grandmother's shoes now that she'd taken over the bakery.

With a thrill of anticipation, she continued walking, her mind already racing with ideas. *What if I volunteered to run a cookie decorating booth? Or organized a baking class for the kids?* The possibilities filled her with excitement, and she almost giggled at the thought of helping with the festival.

As she neared her grandmother's bakery, the familiar scent of vanilla and cinnamon greeted her, enveloping her like a warm hug. She paused in front of the door, gazing at her reflection in the frosted window and whispering, "Oh, Grandma Millie, what would you do?"

The bakery, with its cheery interior and old-fashioned charm, held so many memories for her. Each tray of cookies, each batch of cakes, felt like a connection to her grandmother, and Merry had promised herself she would carry on the legacy. But she also wanted to be part of the broader traditions of Tannenbaum Falls—the same traditions that had drawn her grandmother to the town so many years ago.

Her mind made up, Merry turned away from the bakery, determination guiding her steps toward the town hall. She would make time to volunteer; she'd find a way to manage both her bakery and her duties for the festival.

The town hall stood before her, its stone facade draped with evergreen garlands and lights. Merry took a deep breath, smoothed her sweater, and pushed open the heavy doors. Inside, the energy buzzed as volunteers moved about, some carrying boxes of decorations, others sorting through lists and schedules. At the center of it all stood Mayor Richard Harlow, his rotund figure a familiar sight as he directed the whirlwind of activity.

With a deep breath, Merry approached him, her smile bright with excitement. "Mayor Harlow?" she called out, hoping to catch his attention. "I'm Merry North, the new owner of Millie's Bakery."

The mayor turned, his eyes widening in recognition. "Ah, Miss North!" he greeted warmly, his voice booming in the echoing hall. "Your grandmother spoke of you often. And now you're here, keeping the spirit of her bakery alive. She'd be proud, young lady."

Merry felt her cheeks warm at his kind words. "Thank you, Mayor. I'm doing my best to honor her legacy," she said, a mixture of pride and nostalgia in her voice. "Actually, I was hoping to volunteer for the Christmas festival, if there's still a need."

Mayor Harlow's eyebrows raised with a hint of surprise. "Now, that's the spirit! But running a bakery during the holidays is no small task. Are you sure you're up for the extra work?"

Merry nodded eagerly, her auburn hair bouncing with the movement. "I know it'll be a challenge, but the festival means so much to me. To all of us, really. I want to be part of it."

The mayor's skepticism softened, replaced by a warm smile. "Well, Miss North, we could always use more help. The festival isn't just about decorations and hot cocoa. It's about bringing the town together, and I think you're just the person to help us do that." He gestured to a nearby table stacked with volunteer forms. "If you'd like to join, start here."

Merry's heart swelled with joy as she filled out the form, her mind already spinning with ways she could contribute. *Maybe I could bake treats for the festival,* she thought. *Or host a cookie-decorating booth for the kids.*

When she finished, Mayor Harlow took the form from her and gave her a grateful nod. "Thank you, Miss North. This festival is Tannenbaum Falls' heart and soul, and it means a lot to us to see you getting involved. Your grandmother would be proud."

The mayor's words resonated deeply, and Merry nodded, feeling a surge of pride. "I'd love to help however I can," she said, her smile wide. "Is there anything else that needs special attention?"

Mayor Harlow rubbed his chin thoughtfully. "Actually, we could use some help with the cookie decorating booth. With your background, I imagine you'd be perfect for that."

"Oh, I'd love to!" Merry exclaimed, her mind already swirling with ideas. "I could even bring some of Grandma Millie's old recipes. They were always a hit."

Mayor Harlow's smile crinkled with appreciation. "That would be wonderful. It's nice to see the festival in such good hands."

As she turned to leave, Merry felt a sense of purpose unlike anything she'd felt since taking over the bakery. With a final thank-you to the mayor, she headed back toward Main Street, her heart lighter and her steps quick with excitement.

Outside, the crisp winter air greeted her once more, mingling with the scent of fresh pine and cinnamon. Carolers stood on the corner, their voices harmonizing in "Silent Night," and Merry paused to take it all in. It was like a Christmas card come to life.

Walking back toward her bakery, she noticed the storefronts along Main Street twinkling with decorations, each shop embracing the spirit of the season. The lights above cast a warm glow on the snow-covered sidewalks, and Merry couldn't help but smile at the thought of being part of such a beloved town tradition.

"Miss North!" a voice called from across the street. Merry turned to see Mrs. Henderson, the town's friendly librarian, waving as she crossed over to join her.

Merry's face lit up. "Mrs. Henderson, it's so nice to see you!"

The older woman adjusted her glasses, her face alight with curiosity. "What's got you looking so chipper today?"

"I just signed up to help with the Christmas festival," Merry replied, her excitement bubbling over. "I'll be running the cookie-decorating booth!"

Mrs. Henderson clapped her hands together in delight. "Oh, how wonderful! Your grandmother always spoke of your Christmas spirit. She'd be thrilled to know you're carrying on the tradition."

Touched, Merry felt her heart swell. "Thank you. I just hope I can live up to her legacy."

"Oh, you're already doing that, my dear. And you know, if you'd like, the library could partner with you for a story time and cookie decorating event. I think the children would love it."

Merry's eyes brightened. "That's a fantastic idea! Let's plan it."

They chatted briefly, sharing ideas for the event, and Merry felt even more inspired by the warmth of the community around her. As she continued down the street, nearly everyone she encountered shared in her excitement. Mr. Johnson from the hardware store offered to help set up her booth, and the twins from the craft shop suggested decorations. Even Mr. Grumble, a gruff man known for his lack of holiday cheer, managed a half-smile and a nod.

When she finally reached the bakery, Merry paused once more to savor the moment. She placed her hand on the door handle, inhaling deeply as the familiar scent of vanilla and cinnamon filled her senses.

## A Very Krampus Christmas

"Alright, Grandma Millie," she whispered, her voice soft but determined. "Let's show this town what Christmas spirit really means."

Inside, the warmth of the bakery wrapped around her like a favorite sweater. Rows of cookies lined the counter, waiting to be decorated, and trays of cinnamon rolls cooled on wire racks. She tied on her apron, her heart brimming with joy, and prepared to tackle the day's tasks.

As she measured flour and cracked eggs, her mind continued to drift to the festival. She could already picture the children's faces as they decorated cookies, the laughter filling the air, and the joy that her treats would bring. It was moments like these, she realized, that truly made the holidays special.

"Just one step at a time," she murmured, reaching for the flour with a steady hand. "Just like baking. It all comes together, one ingredient at a time."

She worked with precision, humming a quiet carol as she mixed dough, her thoughts drifting to all the possibilities ahead. The festival felt like a magical thread that connected everyone in town, and she was grateful to be a part of it.

As Merry finished scooping rows of cookie dough onto baking sheets, the front bell jingled, announcing the arrival of her first customer of the day. Looking up, she saw young Sam Petersen, one of her grandmother's old regulars. He was bundled in a scarf and mittens, his cheeks pink from the cold.

"Merry! I didn't think I'd catch you today!" Sam said, his face lighting up at the sight of her.

"Hi, Sam!" Merry greeted him warmly, setting down her spoon. "How's it going? Are you ready for the festival?"

"Oh, yes! My sisters and I are going to help decorate the town tree tomorrow. And I'm so excited for the cookie booth. Mom told me you're running it this year!"

Merry chuckled. "Word travels fast in Tannenbaum Falls. I am indeed! And I'm bringing some special decorations just for you and all the other kids."

"Awesome! I can't wait," Sam replied, practically bouncing with excitement. "We'll make the best-looking cookies ever!"

They chatted for a bit, and Merry sent him off with a gingerbread cookie on the house. Watching him leave, she felt the satisfaction of knowing that she was becoming a part of the town's heart and traditions, just like her grandmother.

Throughout the day, the steady rhythm of baking and decorating filled the hours. Each order that went out brought a sense of purpose and joy, from red-and-green sugar cookies to warm cinnamon rolls, perfect for enjoying with a cup of cocoa. She filled every tray with care, knowing that each treat was destined to bring a smile to someone's face.

By mid-afternoon, Merry took a break, glancing around at her cozy little bakery, and noticed how full it looked with trays of fresh-baked treats and displays decked out in holiday cheer. She poured herself a cup of tea, sitting by the window as the sun began to dip lower in the sky, casting a golden glow over the town square. Just beyond the glass, she could see the townspeople bustling about, adding the final touches to their decorations.

Lost in thought, Merry was startled by a knock at the door. She looked up to see Mayor Harlow, his familiar face grinning through the frosted glass. She quickly waved him in.

"Afternoon, Miss North," he said, closing the door behind him and brushing off a light dusting of snow from his coat. "I hope I'm not interrupting?"

"Not at all, Mayor. Please, have a seat," Merry replied, gesturing to the small table near the window.

He took a seat, his eyes roving appreciatively over the bakery's cozy decorations. "You've done quite a job keeping Millie's charm alive here. It's wonderful to see."

"Thank you," Merry said, her heart swelling with pride. "I just want to make her proud."

The mayor nodded thoughtfully. "I have no doubt you're doing just that. In fact, I came by with a little request, if you're up for it."

Merry tilted her head, intrigued. "Of course! Anything for the festival."

"Well," he began, adjusting his scarf, "we were wondering if you might be interested in preparing some treats for the town's tree lighting ceremony tomorrow night. It's become quite the event, and folks are always delighted to have some of Millie's famous recipes on hand."

Merry's mind whirled with excitement. "I'd be honored! I'll bake up a special batch of holiday cookies and maybe some gingerbread men."

The mayor clapped his hands together, clearly pleased. "Wonderful! You've got a way of making everything feel special, Miss North."

They shared a cup of tea, exchanging stories of past festivals, and Merry could almost feel her grandmother's presence beside her, smiling proudly. After the mayor left, she set to work, her mind focused on creating the perfect treats for tomorrow.

As the sky grew darker, Merry's baking marathon continued. She lost herself in the comforting process of kneading, rolling, and decorating, the familiar routines soothing her as she crafted each batch. Trays filled with stars, trees, and gingerbread figures lined the countertops, each one more festive than the last.

Just as she was placing the final tray in the oven, her phone buzzed with a message from her sister, Lucy.

*Need a taste-tester?* the message read, accompanied by a playful winking emoji.

Merry grinned and quickly typed back, *I thought you'd never ask! Come by when you're ready.*

Fifteen minutes later, Lucy arrived, bundled up in a wool coat and beanie, her cheeks rosy from the cold. She swept into the bakery, pulling her gloves off and sighing with relief as the warmth enveloped her.

"Oh, Merry, this place smells like Christmas itself," she exclaimed, inhaling deeply.

"That's the idea," Merry laughed, setting a freshly baked tray of gingerbread men on the counter. "How about a taste test?"

Lucy's eyes sparkled with delight as she reached for a cookie. "You know me too well. I'll never say no to one of your creations."

They spent the next hour together, sampling cookies and laughing over childhood memories of Christmas in Tannenbaum Falls. As they reminisced, Merry felt her worries about balancing the bakery and the festival begin to fade. Lucy's presence was a reminder of the magic of family and the joy of the holidays, and it grounded her in her purpose.

"I can't wait to see your booth at the festival," Lucy said as she took a sip of hot cocoa. "You're going to bring so much joy to everyone, Merry. Just like Grandma did."

The sentiment filled Merry with a renewed sense of purpose. "Thank you, Lucy. I'll give it my all, that's for sure."

By the time Lucy left, the bakery was quiet and still, the only sound the soft hum of the oven as it finished the final batch of cookies. Merry glanced around, admiring the rows of treats she'd created. Tomorrow, she'd share them with the town, spreading the love and joy she'd poured into each one.

As she closed up shop, she felt a peaceful satisfaction settle over her. The festival was just beginning, but already she felt like she was a part of something truly special.

The next evening, the town square was abuzz with excitement. Merry arrived early, her car loaded with boxes of cookies, gingerbread men, and holiday treats for the ceremony. She carefully set up her booth, arranging platters of cookies and baskets of candy canes, adding festive red and green ribbons to complete the display.

The air was crisp, and the town square glowed under strings of lights that crisscrossed overhead, casting a warm glow over the excited crowd. Families gathered, children laughing as they ran between the booths, their voices blending with the familiar tunes of carolers singing nearby.

Merry's heart swelled with pride as she looked around, taking in the sights and sounds of the festival. It was everything she'd dreamed it would be—a joyful celebration that brought everyone together, just as her grandmother had always described.

As people began to line up at her booth, Merry offered warm smiles and handed out cookies, each treat met with delighted gasps and words of appreciation. She shared a few of her grandmother's recipes with curious bakers and watched as children carefully decorated gingerbread men with icing and sprinkles, their faces lit with concentration.

At the center of the square, the town's enormous Christmas tree sparkled with ornaments, and a hush fell over the crowd as Mayor Harlow stepped forward to begin the ceremony. He spoke warmly about the festival's history, the importance of tradition, and the spirit of togetherness that defined Tannenbaum Falls.

Merry stood in the crowd, her heart full as she listened, a sense of belonging wrapping around her like a cozy blanket. When the lights on the tree were finally switched on, the crowd erupted in applause, the tree's glow illuminating their smiling faces.

## A Very Krampus Christmas

As the festivities continued, Merry found herself surrounded by friends, neighbors, and loved ones, all of them sharing in the joy she'd worked so hard to create. She spotted Lucy waving from across the square, holding a gingerbread man decorated with a grin.

For a moment, Merry closed her eyes, taking in the laughter, the music, and the scent of pine and cinnamon filling the air. In that instant, she knew she was exactly where she was meant to be.

The festival was just one night, but the memories would last forever. And as she stood under the glow of the Christmas tree, surrounded by the warmth of her community, Merry felt certain that her grandmother was there, smiling down on her with pride

## Chapter 3

The bell over the door chimed cheerfully as Merry stepped into Beverly's Trinkets and Treasures, and her heart gave an unexpected leap at the sight of Klaus Krampus standing by the counter, engaged in lively conversation with Beverly. Strings of holiday lights sparkled overhead, and the inviting scent of cinnamon filled the air, but Merry barely noticed, her attention drawn entirely to Klaus's tall figure and his slightly tousled dark hair, which looked as if he'd been running his hands through it.

She took a steadying breath, brushing an imaginary wrinkle from her sweater as she thought, *You've known him forever; it's just Klaus.* Gathering her courage, she moved forward with a bright smile. "Beverly! Klaus! It's so good to see you both."

Beverly's face brightened, her cheerful energy palpable. "Merry, darling! We were just talking about you—and those mouth-watering cookies of yours."

Klaus turned at her approach, his smile warm. "Merry. It's been too long."

The deep timbre of his voice sent a pleasant shiver down Merry's spine. She tucked a loose strand of hair behind her ear, hoping her cheeks weren't giving away her excitement. "It really has," she replied, doing her best to sound casual. "How have you been? Still keeping busy in that workshop of yours?"

A low chuckle escaped Klaus, filling the cozy shop. "You know me too well. The elves make sure I don't have too many idle hours, but I wouldn't have it any other way."

Beverly clapped her hands, clearly delighted. "Oh, it does my heart good to see you two catching up! Merry, how's the bakery treating you? I hear you've been working wonders with your grandmother's recipes."

Merry's initial nervousness faded into pride as she responded, "It's been a whirlwind, but I love it. I'm doing everything I can to keep Grandma's legacy alive."

"From what I've heard, you're more than succeeding," Klaus said, his tone gentle. "Your grandmother always believed you had a little magic in your fingers when it came to baking."

The words warmed Merry's heart. She cast a grateful look around the shop, taking in the cozy decorations that filled every corner. "Beverly, you've really outdone yourself this year. The shop looks like something out of a Christmas story."

Beverly beamed, adjusting her colorful scarf. "Thank you, dear. But I must say, Klaus's ornaments really add a touch of magic." She patted his shoulder affectionately before launching into a story about her recent crafting mishap with a particularly stubborn glue gun.

While Beverly animatedly described her glue-related misadventures, Merry found herself glancing at Klaus more often than she intended. He seemed softer somehow, as if time had worn away some of the mystery that had always surrounded him. She couldn't help but wonder what had changed for him in the years she'd been away.

"So, Merry," Klaus said, his voice breaking into her thoughts, "what's new? Besides becoming the town's premier cookie expert, of course."

"Oh, you know," Merry replied, grateful for the easy flow of conversation, "just trying to keep up with Grandma's legacy without burning down the kitchen."

They shared a laugh, and Merry felt a familiar warmth spreading through her chest. Coming back to Tannenbaum Falls had felt like a leap of faith, but in moments like this, she couldn't imagine being anywhere else.

A comfortable silence fell between them, but Klaus's expression shifted to something thoughtful, his voice lowering as he began, "Do you remember that Christmas Eve when we got snowed in at the old Miller barn?"

Merry's cheeks flushed at the memory. "How could I forget? We spent the whole night telling ghost stories and drinking hot cocoa from that old thermos of yours."

Klaus's smile broadened. "And you were certain the barn was haunted by Old Man Miller's spirit."

"Those creaky floorboards didn't help!" she protested, laughing despite the flutter in her stomach at the shared memory. The moment was charged, holding something unspoken that tugged at her heart, sparking thoughts of what might have been if she hadn't left town years ago.

Klaus cleared his throat, breaking the silence. "Well, down to business. The festival won't plan itself."

Grateful for the shift in topic, Merry nodded eagerly. "Right, of course. What's the plan?"

Klaus's expression turned serious, his passion evident as he explained, "The key is involving the entire community. I want everyone to feel like they're part of something special."

Merry's eyes lit up at the idea. "I couldn't agree more. This town thrives on community, especially during the holidays."

"That's what I thought, too," Klaus replied, his gaze softening. "I was hoping you'd have some ideas on how to bring that spirit to life."

"Well," Merry began, the excitement bubbling within her as her hands moved expressively, "I was thinking we could carry on the cookie tradition my grandmother started. We could set up a decorating station for the kids, where they can add their own creative touches to her famous sugar cookies. It would be a perfect way for families to share in the fun."

Klaus nodded, his smile encouraging. "That sounds perfect, Merry. Her cookies were legendary. What else do you have in mind?"

"Maybe a hot chocolate station beside the cookie table?" Merry suggested, her mind racing. "My grandmother had a secret hot chocolate recipe that everyone loved. We could make it a cozy corner for families to warm up."

"That's exactly what we need," Klaus agreed. "A spot where people can linger, laugh, and make memories. I was also thinking of setting up different activity stations throughout the square—gift-wrapping, ornament making, maybe even a spot for kids to write letters to Santa."

A surge of nostalgia mixed with excitement rose in Merry. "That's perfect! It captures the spirit of Tannenbaum Falls beautifully." She paused, then added with a grin, "And maybe we should add a little carol-singing corner too, so people can belt out 'Jingle Bells' without hesitation."

## A Very Krampus Christmas

Klaus laughed, clearly loving the idea. "You know, for someone who's always teased me about being a bit of a Grinch, you're awfully enthusiastic about this festival. Are you sure you're not secretly a Christmas elf?"

"Oh, absolutely," Merry said, playing along. "But if I'm an elf, that must make you Santa."

Klaus chuckled, shaking his head. "I think my beard-growing skills might leave a bit to be desired. But your delightful cookies will be the main attraction, so maybe we'll leave the Santa duties to someone else."

Before Merry could respond, Beverly appeared with a tray of steaming mugs. "Hot cocoa, anyone?" She gave them a mischievous grin. "It's my special recipe. Guaranteed to put some cheer in your holiday planning."

Merry accepted a mug gratefully, inhaling the warm aroma of cocoa mingling with the shop's cinnamon-scented air. "This is exactly what we need, Beverly. Thank you."

They all took a sip, and Klaus sighed contentedly. "You've really created something magical here, Beverly. This shop is like stepping into a winter wonderland."

Beverly's face glowed with pride. "Why, thank you, Klaus! That means a lot coming from the master of Christmas magic himself." She gave Merry a wink. "Now, if only we could get you both to try on these costumes." Beverly held up a Santa beard and a jingle bell hat. "Just for fun?"

Klaus held up a hand in mock protest. "I'm afraid I'd scare the children away more than I'd delight them." But his laughter showed he was more amused than horrified.

Merry laughed along, imagining Klaus decked out as Santa, jingle bells and all. "Only if you agree to be one of my elves, Klaus. I think you'd look dashing in pointy shoes and a green hat."

The laughter in the shop grew, mingling with the soft holiday music playing in the background. Merry found herself wiping away tears of mirth, feeling lighter than she had in ages. As her laughter faded, she noticed Klaus watching her, a fond smile tugging at his lips. For a moment, the world around them seemed to pause, and a soft warmth settled in her chest.

Klaus's expression softened, and he said quietly, "Your grandmother would be proud, Merry. The way you're embracing these traditions, making them your own... it's inspiring."

Merry's heart swelled at his words. "Thank you, Klaus. That really means a lot."

Their eyes met, and in that brief, shared moment, Merry felt as if an invisible thread connected them, woven from the memories of winters past and the promise of something more. The spell was broken when the bell over the door jingled, signaling the arrival of a customer. Merry took a small step back, suddenly aware of how close they'd been standing.

She cleared her throat, gathering her thoughts. "So, about the festival. I think we've made some good progress today."

Klaus nodded, his gaze lingering on her. "Definitely. But there's still a lot to discuss."

"Agreed," Merry said, feeling a flutter of excitement at the thought of seeing him again. "Maybe we can meet tomorrow to go over more details?"

"I'd like that," Klaus replied, a hint of a smile returning. "How about at the gazebo in the town square? Say, around two?"

Merry's heart gave a little leap. "Perfect. I'll see you then."

As they finalized their plans, Merry became acutely aware of the festive warmth around them in Beverly's shop. The gentle hum of Christmas music mingled with the glow of holiday lights, and the cinnamon-scented air reminded her of cozy nights spent baking with her grandmother.

Beverly, noticing the lingering atmosphere between them, cheerfully handed each of them a candy cane, beaming as she said, "Nothing says Christmas like a little peppermint! Go on, add it to your hot cocoa." She waved them off as Merry slipped on her coat.

Klaus's rich laugh warmed the space between them as he hooked his candy cane over the rim of his mug. "Beverly knows just how to keep us in the holiday spirit," he said, giving her a nod of thanks.

As they headed toward the door, Merry wrapped her scarf tighter around her neck, preparing for the cold outside. Klaus held the door open for her, and she stepped out into the brisk winter evening, the scent of pine and fresh snow filling her lungs. Klaus followed, his expression thoughtful as he glanced at the glittering snowflakes dusting the shop's front window.

For a moment, they stood side by side on the sidewalk, taking in the peaceful quiet of Tannenbaum Falls in the evening. A gentle hush had fallen over the town square, with only a few stragglers finishing their holiday shopping or pausing to listen to the carolers' last verses of "O Holy Night."

Merry felt a wave of gratitude wash over her. "Thanks for today, Klaus. I'm really looking forward to the festival now," she said, her voice softer than usual.

Klaus turned to face her, his breath visible in the cold night air. "It's been good to work on something like this with you, Merry. I think your grandmother would be proud to see how you're making her traditions your own." His words held a sincerity that made her feel both vulnerable and valued.

They shared a quiet look, one filled with mutual respect, friendship, and perhaps a hint of something more.

"Well, I better head back to the bakery," Merry said with a smile, breaking the silence. "There's a batch of gingerbread men waiting for me."

Klaus chuckled, his warm expression never wavering. "I'll look forward to sampling them at the festival. Your grandmother's recipes have a way of making Christmas feel more complete."

"Then I'll make sure to bring extra," she said, grinning.

With a final nod, Klaus began walking toward his workshop, while Merry turned down the familiar path to her bakery, her thoughts lingering on the day's events. The town square was quiet, blanketed in freshly fallen snow that sparkled under the lamplights. The distant hum of holiday music echoed in the night, and Merry found herself humming along, feeling as if a little bit of magic had settled over her.

As she neared her bakery, she paused, looking up at the stars dotting the night sky. "Oh, Grandma," she whispered, "I hope I'm making you proud."

Inside the bakery, the familiar warmth enveloped her, and the comforting aroma of cinnamon and vanilla filled the air. She shrugged off her coat, tied on her apron, and set to work, the rhythm of baking soothing her lingering thoughts of Klaus. As she mixed the gingerbread dough, memories of their shared laughter and nostalgia surfaced, filling her with a sense of anticipation she hadn't felt in years.

The following day, Merry found herself back in the bustling town square, her heart skipping a beat as she approached the gazebo where Klaus had suggested they meet. The air was crisp, and a soft blanket of snow covered the ground, making everything feel fresh and new. Wreaths adorned the gazebo's railings, and festive ribbons trailed down from its peak, giving it an extra touch of holiday cheer.

Klaus was already there, leaning casually against one of the posts, a notebook in hand. His expression brightened when he spotted her approaching.

"Merry," he greeted, tucking the notebook under his arm. "Right on time."

"Wouldn't miss it," she replied, settling into the spot beside him on the gazebo bench.

They immediately began talking about the plans for the festival, bouncing ideas off one another with ease. Merry could feel the excitement building as they discussed every little detail, from the placement of booths to the layout of the cookie station.

"So, for the cookie decorating booth," Merry said, "I was thinking we could add some extra touches—maybe holiday-themed aprons for the kids to wear while they decorate. That way, they'll feel like little bakers for the day."

Klaus's grin grew. "You're really making this special, Merry. I can picture it now. The kids will love it."

A warm flush crept up her neck at his praise, and she responded with a smile. "I just want everyone to feel the magic that I felt here growing up."

They continued sketching out the plans for each station, occasionally pausing to laugh at Klaus's quick-witted commentary. His passion for the festival was evident, and it made her admire him even more.

As they wrapped up their planning session, Klaus closed his notebook, glancing out over the square. "Thank you, Merry. For all of this. I know you've got a lot on your plate, but you're giving this festival everything you've got."

"I wouldn't have it any other way," Merry replied, her gaze following his out to the square where children played in the snow and townspeople decorated lampposts with more greenery and ribbons. "Tannenbaum Falls is home. It deserves a little magic."

Klaus looked back at her, a hint of warmth lingering in his expression. "I think you're bringing plenty of that already."

They fell silent, content to sit together, wrapped in the peacefulness of the moment. The sounds of the town around them created a comforting backdrop, and the soft snow began to fall once more, dusting the gazebo in delicate flakes. For a moment, Merry allowed herself to imagine what it might be like to share more moments like this with Klaus—to experience the holidays, to create traditions together.

But she quickly brushed the thought aside. There was work to be done, after all, and she couldn't let herself get distracted. Standing, she tucked her notes into her bag and turned to Klaus. "Thanks for the help, Klaus. I'll start prepping everything on my end."

Klaus stood as well, giving her a reassuring nod. "I'm here to help if you need it, Merry. Don't hesitate to ask."

Their parting felt reluctant, as if neither quite wanted to leave the comfort of the shared planning session. But Merry forced herself to smile, offering a small wave before she turned and began her walk back toward the bakery, her heart lighter than it had been in a long time.

As the week went on, the preparations for the festival moved full steam ahead. Merry threw herself into the work with enthusiasm, baking countless batches of cookies, arranging frosting in all shades of red and green, and gathering supplies for the hot chocolate station. Each day, she visited the square to oversee the setup, and she often found herself crossing paths with Klaus.

One evening, while she was finishing up the last of the cookie batches, the bell over the bakery door rang, and Klaus walked in, a faint dusting of snow clinging to his coat. He gave her a warm smile as he set down a box on the counter.

"Thought you could use these," he said, opening the box to reveal dozens of handmade wooden ornaments, each one carved with care and precision. "For the tree-trimming station. Figured you'd want something special."

Merry's hand flew to her mouth, moved by the gesture. "Klaus, these are beautiful. They're exactly what we needed." She ran her fingers over one of the ornaments, a delicate star, feeling the smooth wood beneath her fingers.

"Glad you like them," he replied softly, watching her reaction. "Just thought I'd add a little something to the event."

They worked side by side for the rest of the evening, arranging the ornaments and preparing the supplies. The warmth of the bakery, combined with Klaus's quiet presence, created a cozy, contented atmosphere, and Merry found herself wishing the moment wouldn't end.

As they finished, Klaus leaned against the counter, a slight smile on his face. "You know, it's been a while since I've seen someone bring this much joy to the festival."

Merry met his gaze, the sincerity in his words touching her deeply. "I just want everyone to feel as much at home as I do here. It's a special place."

Klaus nodded, his voice softening. "It certainly is. And I'm glad you're here to remind us of that."

They shared a lingering look, and for a moment, Merry felt her heart quicken. But then the clock struck eight, signaling the end of another busy day. Taking a deep breath, she stepped back, pulling her coat on as she prepared to leave.

"See you at the festival tomorrow?" she asked, giving him a warm smile.

Klaus's expression softened. "I wouldn't miss it."

With one last wave, Merry stepped out into the snowy night, the quiet stillness wrapping around her. She made her way home, her heart full, excitement fluttering in her chest for the day to come.

The festival was nearly here, and as she walked through the snow-covered streets of Tannenbaum Falls, Merry knew it was going to be a Christmas she'd remember forever.

# Chapter 4

Merry's heart fluttered as she stepped over the threshold of Clara Miller's quaint cottage. The scent of cinnamon and pine enveloped her, instantly soothing her nerves. She took a deep breath, savoring the comforting aroma that reminded her of childhood Christmases.

"Merry, dear! Come in, come in!" Clara's warm voice rang out as she shuffled towards the door, her eyes twinkling with delight. "I'm so glad you could make it."

Merry smiled, feeling some of her apprehension melt away. "Thank you for having me, Clara. Your home is lovely."

Clara waved a hand dismissively, but Merry could see the pride in her eyes. "Oh, it's just a little place. But it's home." She gestured towards the living room. "Why don't you have a seat by the fire? It's dreadfully chilly out there today."

Merry nodded gratefully and made her way to the overstuffed armchair near the fireplace. As she sank into its plush cushions, she couldn't help but feel a sense of belonging. The crackling flames cast a warm glow across the room, illuminating shelves filled with well-worn books and cheerful knick-knacks.

"This is so cozy," Merry said, her voice filled with genuine appreciation. "I can see why you love it here."

Clara chuckled as she lowered herself into the chair opposite Merry. "It's not much, but it's perfect for an old soul like me." She leaned forward, her eyes twinkling. "Now, tell me, how are you settling in at the bakery? I bet it feels like coming home, doesn't it?"

Merry's heart swelled with affection for this kind woman who seemed to understand her so well. She found herself relaxing further into the chair, the uncertainty that had plagued her earlier beginning to fade away in the warmth of Clara's presence and the comforting atmosphere of the cottage.

Clara's gentle smile encouraged Merry to open up. "You know, it really does feel like coming home," Merry began, her green eyes misting with nostalgia. "I remember as a little girl, the scent of Grandma's gingerbread cookies would fill the entire street. It was like a beacon calling everyone to the bakery."

Clara nodded, her eyes crinkling at the corners. "Oh, I remember those cookies! Your grandmother had a magic touch with spices. Tell me more about your favorite holiday memories here in Tannenbaum Falls."

Merry's face lit up as she recalled, "The annual tree lighting ceremony was always my favorite. We'd all gather in the town square, sipping hot cocoa and singing carols. And when that giant spruce lit up..." She trailed off, lost in the memory.

"It was like the whole town was holding its breath," Clara chimed in, her voice warm with shared recollection. "And then, when those lights flickered on, it was pure magic."

Merry nodded enthusiastically. "Exactly! I used to think actual fairies had come to light up the tree." She laughed softly, a touch embarrassed at her childhood fancy.

Clara leaned forward, her eyes twinkling. "Who's to say they didn't? This town has always had a touch of magic about it, especially during Christmas."

As Merry shared more memories - decorating the bakery window, sledding down Pinecone Hill, the yearly snowman-building contest - she felt a warmth spreading through her chest. It wasn't just from the crackling fire; it was the feeling of reconnecting with a part of herself she'd almost forgotten.

Merry's smile faltered slightly as she finished recounting her memories. She fidgeted with the hem of her sweater, a small sigh escaping her lips. Clara's keen eyes caught the shift in Merry's demeanor, and she reached out to pat Merry's hand gently.

"My dear," Clara said, her voice soft and reassuring, "I can see these traditions mean a great deal to you. They're not just memories; they're the very threads that weave your family's legacy into the fabric of Tannenbaum Falls."

## A Very Krampus Christmas

Merry looked up, her green eyes shimmering with a mix of emotions. "It's just... it feels like so much responsibility. What if I can't live up to it all?"

Clara's wise eyes crinkled at the corners as she smiled. "Embracing the holiday spirit isn't about perfection, Merry. It's about finding joy in the little moments, in the traditions that have shaped your family for generations."

As if to punctuate her point, Clara rose from her chair with surprising agility for her age. "I think this calls for a cup of tea," she announced, moving towards a beautifully carved wooden cabinet.

Merry watched as Clara retrieved an ornate teapot, painted with delicate snowflakes. "That's beautiful," she murmured, admiring the craftsmanship.

"A gift from your grandmother, actually," Clara said, her eyes twinkling. "She always said a good cup of tea could solve most of life's problems."

As Clara busied herself with the tea, Merry found herself relaxing, the cozy ambiance of the cottage wrapping around her like a warm blanket. The gentle clink of china and the soft whistle of the kettle filled the air, mingling with the crackling of the fire.

"You know," Merry said, her voice thoughtful, "Gram always made hot chocolate for me when I was feeling overwhelmed. I guess some traditions never change, do they?"

Clara turned, two steaming cups in hand, the rich aroma of cinnamon and cloves wafting through the air. "Indeed they don't, my dear. And that's the beauty of it all."

Clara settled back into her chair, cradling her teacup. "Speaking of traditions," she began, her eyes twinkling with memories, "did you know Tannenbaum Falls used to host the grandest Winter Solstice Festival in the entire county?"

Merry leaned forward, intrigued. "Really? I don't think I've ever heard about that."

"Oh, it was a sight to behold," Clara said, her voice rich with nostalgia. "The town square would be transformed into a winter wonderland. Ice sculptures, carolers on every corner, and a magnificent bonfire that burned all night long."

Merry closed her eyes, trying to picture the scene. "It sounds magical," she murmured.

"It truly was," Clara agreed. "And your grandmother's cookies were always the star attraction. People would line up for hours just to get a taste."

A warm glow of pride bloomed in Merry's chest. "I had no idea," she said softly.

Clara nodded, her eyes distant with remembrance. "The festival brought everyone together. It wasn't just about the spectacle, you see. It was about community, about sharing in the joy of the season."

Merry sipped her tea, savoring the blend of spices. "What happened to the festival?" she asked.

"Times changed," Clara sighed. "People got busier, traditions fell by the wayside. But the spirit of it lives on in smaller ways - in the Christmas market, the tree lighting ceremony."

Fascinated, Merry found herself hungry for more. "You seem to know so much about the town's history, Clara. How did you become the keeper of all these stories?"

Clara's eyes sparkled. "Well, my dear, that's a story in itself. You see, it all started when I was just a young girl, not much older than you..."

As Clara launched into her tale, Merry settled deeper into her chair, captivated. She felt a growing connection to this town, to its rich tapestry of traditions and memories. And for the first time since arriving in Tannenbaum Falls, she felt like she truly belonged.

Clara leaned forward, her eyes twinkling with a youthful exuberance that belied her age. "You see, Merry, the magic of Tannenbaum Falls isn't just in the twinkling lights or the festive decorations. It's in the way people come together, sharing their warmth and love with one another."

Merry nodded, feeling a surge of emotion as she recognized the truth in Clara's words. The older woman continued, her voice soft but passionate.

"During the holidays, we're reminded of what truly matters. It's not about the presents under the tree, but the presence of loved ones around it. The way a simple act of kindness can light up someone's day brighter than any string of Christmas lights."

As Clara spoke, Merry found herself transported. She could almost hear the laughter of children sledding down snow-covered hills, smell the aroma of fresh-baked cookies wafting from open windows, feel the warmth of friendly embraces exchanged on street corners.

"It sounds wonderful," Merry murmured, her voice thick with longing.

Clara reached out, patting Merry's hand gently. "It is, my dear. And you know, speaking of connections..." She paused, her expression turning thoughtful. "Have you had a chance to catch up with Klaus since you've been back?"

Merry's breath caught in her throat. "Klaus? I... well, not really. We've bumped into each other a couple of times, but..."

"Ah, Klaus," Clara sighed, a knowing smile playing on her lips. "You two always had such a special bond. The way you'd decorate the town square together, or how he'd save the best wooden ornaments for your family's tree."

Memories flooded back, bittersweet and vivid. Merry found herself transported to crisp winter evenings, the scent of pine in the air, Klaus's laughter ringing out as they hung garlands and strings of lights.

"Perhaps," Clara suggested gently, "it might be worth rekindling that connection. The holidays have a way of bringing people together, after all."

Merry bit her lip, a mix of emotions swirling within her. "Do you really think so?" she asked, her voice barely above a whisper.

Merry's heart skipped a beat at the mention of Klaus. She fidgeted with the hem of her sweater, her gaze dropping to the steaming cup of tea in front of her. The warmth of the fireplace suddenly felt too intense, mirroring the flush creeping up her cheeks.

"I... I don't know, Clara," Merry confessed, her voice trembling slightly. "There's so much history there, so many what-ifs." She lifted her eyes, meeting Clara's understanding gaze. "Part of me wants to reach out, to see if there's still a spark, but I'm scared. What if too much time has passed? What if we've both changed too much?"

Clara leaned forward, her weathered hands clasping Merry's. "My dear, change is as natural as the seasons. It doesn't erase the connections we've made; it only adds new layers to them."

Merry nodded, feeling a lump form in her throat. "I want to be happy, to feel fulfilled. But it's not just about Klaus. I'm still trying to find my footing here, to make the bakery a success, to live up to Grandma's legacy. It all feels so overwhelming sometimes."

"Ah, but that's the beauty of it," Clara said, her eyes twinkling. "Love and personal growth aren't separate paths, Merry. They intertwine, supporting each other like the branches of our beloved tannenbaums."

Merry couldn't help but smile at the comparison. "You really think it's not too late? To pursue... well, everything?"

Clara's laugh was warm and reassuring. "My dear, it's never too late to follow your heart's desires. The path to happiness isn't always straight or clear, but every step you take brings you closer."

As their conversation drew to a close, Clara rose from her chair with a soft groan, her joints creaking slightly. She shuffled over to an antique wooden cabinet, its surface adorned with intricate carvings of pine trees and snowflakes. Merry watched curiously as Clara opened a small drawer and withdrew a package no larger than her palm, wrapped in shimmering silver paper and tied with a delicate red ribbon.

"I have something for you, dear," Clara said, her eyes twinkling as she returned to her seat. She held out the gift to Merry, who accepted it with trembling hands.

"Oh, Clara, you didn't have to—" Merry began, but Clara waved her off with a gentle smile.

"Go on, open it," she encouraged.

Merry carefully untied the ribbon and peeled back the paper, revealing a small, ornate wooden box. As she lifted the lid, a soft tinkling melody filled the air—a familiar Christmas tune that tugged at her heartstrings.

"It's beautiful," Merry breathed, her eyes filling with tears. "Is this...?"

Clara nodded. "The very same tune that played at the town's first Christmas festival. I thought it might serve as a reminder of the joy and possibilities that await you here in Tannenbaum Falls."

Merry closed the box gently, clutching it to her chest. "Thank you, Clara. For this, for everything. I don't know how to express how much your guidance means to me."

"You don't need to, dear," Clara replied warmly. "Your smile says it all."

As Merry stood to leave, she felt a renewed sense of purpose coursing through her veins. The weight of uncertainty that had been pressing down on her shoulders seemed to lift, replaced by a flutter of excitement in her chest.

## A Very Krampus Christmas

"I think... I think I'm ready to embrace this holiday season," Merry said, her voice growing stronger with each word. "And maybe... maybe it's time I reached out to Klaus."

Clara's eyes crinkled with joy. "That's the spirit, my dear. Remember, the magic of Christmas isn't just in the air—it's in our hearts, waiting to be awakened."

Merry nodded, feeling a warmth spread through her that had nothing to do with the crackling fire. As she gathered her coat, she realized that for the first time since arriving in Tannenbaum Falls, she felt truly at home.

Merry stepped out of Clara's cottage, the crisp winter air nipping at her cheeks and bringing a rosy glow to her face. The small package Clara had given her nestled snugly in her coat pocket, a comforting weight against her side. As she made her way down the snow-dusted path, her mind buzzed with possibilities.

"I can't believe I'm actually considering this," Merry murmured to herself, her breath forming little clouds in the frosty air. She paused, gazing up at the twinkling lights strung between the quaint shops lining the street. The sight filled her with a warmth that spread from her heart to her fingertips.

Just then, the cheerful jingle of sleigh bells caught her attention. Merry turned to see Klaus guiding his horse-drawn carriage down the street, his familiar red cap perched jauntily on his head. Her heart skipped a beat as their eyes met.

Klaus reined in his horses, his face breaking into a wide smile. "Merry! What a pleasant surprise. Care for a ride back to the bakery?"

Merry hesitated for a moment, Clara's words echoing in her mind. Taking a deep breath, she stepped forward. "You know what? I'd love one."

As she climbed into the carriage, Klaus's strong hand steadying her, Merry felt a rush of warmth that had nothing to do with the cozy blanket he draped over her lap. She settled in beside him, acutely aware of his presence.

"So, how was your visit with Clara?" Klaus asked, urging the horses forward with a gentle flick of the reins.

Merry's fingers brushed against the package in her pocket. "It was... enlightening," she replied, a small smile playing on her lips. "Clara has a way of putting things into perspective."

Klaus chuckled, the sound rich and warm. "That she does. Did she share any of her famous gingerbread cookies with you?"

"No, but she did give me something to think about," Merry said, her voice softening. She turned to look at Klaus, really look at him, and found herself captivated by the kindness in his eyes. "Klaus, I've been wondering... would you like to help me decorate the bakery for Christmas? I could use an expert's touch."

As the words left her mouth, Merry felt a mix of nervousness and excitement. This was it—her first step towards something new, something potentially wonderful.

Klaus's face lit up, his smile brighter than all the Christmas lights in Tannenbaum Falls. "I'd be honored, Merry. There's nothing I'd love more."

As they rode through the twinkling streets, Merry's heart felt as light as freshly fallen snow. She had taken the first step, and the path ahead, while uncertain, sparkled with promise.

## Chapter 5

The smell of cinnamon and pine greeted Merry as she stepped into the bustling community center. She glanced around, soaking in the festive decorations and a room full of neighbors in cheerful conversation. She took a steadying breath, clutching her notepad with purpose.

"Welcome!" A volunteer at the entrance waved her over. "You must be Merry. So glad you could join us."

"Thank you!" Merry replied, matching the volunteer's warmth. "I'm excited to help with the festival planning."

As she found an empty seat, she noticed how quickly the room filled up, familiar faces all around her. Her grandmother had often talked about these meetings and the sense of community they created. Merry couldn't help but feel a swell of nostalgia as she settled in.

"Alright, everyone, let's get started," called the committee chair, an older woman named Martha who had a commanding but friendly presence. "We have plenty to cover if we want this Winter Wonderland Festival to outshine last year's."

Just as Martha began to speak, the door opened with a quiet creak, and the room fell silent. A man entered, and though he said nothing, his presence alone commanded attention. He looked to be in his seventies, with a neatly groomed gray beard and an air of calm authority. He wore a well-worn tweed jacket, adding to his dignified look.

Martha broke into a warm smile. "Arthur! Glad you could make it."

Arthur nodded, a faint smile softening his otherwise serious expression. "Wouldn't miss it for the world, Martha," he replied in a low, steady voice.

Merry watched him, curiosity sparking. She leaned toward the woman beside her and whispered, "Who is he?"

Her neighbor's eyes widened slightly. "That's Arthur Schmidt, our resident woodcarver. His Christmas ornaments are practically legendary around here. Didn't your grandmother ever mention him?"

Merry nodded, suddenly remembering the stories her grandmother had shared about the beautiful, intricate ornaments that Arthur crafted. She hadn't realized he was such a prominent figure in Tannenbaum Falls.

As the meeting resumed, ideas flew around the room. People discussed food stalls, games for children, and the layout of the square. Merry listened intently, jotting down notes, but her mind kept drifting back to Arthur. There was something captivating about him, something that went beyond his reputation as a craftsman.

When the meeting adjourned, Merry saw her chance. She approached Arthur as he gathered his things, heart thumping with a mix of admiration and nerves.

"Mr. Schmidt?" she began, her voice coming out softer than she'd intended. She cleared her throat and tried again. "Mr. Schmidt, I'm Merry North. I've recently moved here to open the bakery. I just wanted to say how much I admire your work."

Arthur looked up, studying her with a thoughtful expression. "Ah, Miss North, the baker. You've taken over where Ellen used to run things, haven't you?"

"Yes, that's right," Merry replied with a smile. "My grandmother spoke so highly of you. She said your ornaments brought her so much joy every Christmas."

"Your grandmother had a kind heart," he said, his tone softening. "I'm glad my work brings people happiness."

Merry felt her cheeks warm. "Actually, I was wondering…" She hesitated, unsure if her request would seem too forward. But she took a breath and continued. "Would it be possible to visit your workshop sometime? I'd love to see your process and learn more about your craft."

Arthur considered her request, tapping a finger on the notebook he was about to pack away. "I don't usually open my workshop to visitors," he admitted, "but I sense you'd appreciate it. Perhaps this afternoon?"

"Oh, I'd be honored!" Merry's excitement bubbled over. She quickly collected herself, adding, "Thank you, Mr. Schmidt. I'll look forward to it."

Later that afternoon, Merry arrived at Arthur's workshop, a small building tucked behind his home on the edge of town. She knocked, and Arthur opened the door, gesturing for her to step inside.

Merry's senses were instantly enveloped by the rich, earthy scent of pine and beeswax. Dust motes floated in the soft light filtering through narrow windows, casting a golden glow on the wooden workbenches. The rhythmic scrape of sandpaper against wood filled the space, and Merry's own heartbeat seemed to settle into the same calming rhythm.

"It's like stepping into another world," she murmured, gazing around in awe.

Arthur smiled faintly. "It's where I spend most of my time," he said. "A place doesn't need much to feel like home."

Merry wandered deeper into the workshop, taking in the various tools neatly arranged on the walls and the shelves lined with delicate, hand-carved ornaments. She reached out to touch one—a snowflake with intricate lace-like patterns carved into each arm.

"These are incredible," she whispered. "They're even more beautiful up close."

"Years of practice, I suppose," Arthur replied, picking up a piece of wood from his workbench. "It's all in the patience. You take your time, listen to what the wood wants to become."

Merry watched him as he ran his hands over the unfinished piece, his fingers moving with a familiarity that spoke of decades of work. Inspired, an idea began to form in her mind.

"Mr. Schmidt," she ventured, "I was thinking about the festival. What if we used your ornaments as part of the decorations? Maybe even as centerpieces for the main stage?"

Arthur raised an eyebrow, considering her suggestion. "I'd thought about contributing a few ornaments here and there," he admitted. "But do you think people would care for something so... old-fashioned?"

Merry shook her head enthusiastically. "They absolutely would. Your ornaments are the spirit of Christmas, Mr. Schmidt. I think people would love to see them up close. They add such a warmth that you can't get with store-bought decorations."

Arthur studied her for a moment, then nodded slowly. "You seem to have a good head on your shoulders, Miss North. Perhaps we could do more with it. Maybe even create a display that lets people get a real sense of the craftsmanship."

Merry's face lit up. "Yes, that's exactly what I was thinking! We could set up a little area where people can admire the ornaments. Maybe even a small woodcarving demonstration?"

Arthur rubbed his chin, looking thoughtful. "I'm not sure about being the center of attention," he confessed. "But a small demonstration... that could be worthwhile. Children, especially—they might find it interesting."

Merry grinned, her enthusiasm bubbling over. "Oh, absolutely! And it would give visitors something to remember. They'd get to take home a part of Tannenbaum Falls."

Arthur nodded, warming to the idea. "We could even offer some custom ornaments, if you think people would like that."

"They'd love it!" Merry replied without hesitation. She could already picture families admiring Arthur's work, marveling at the craftsmanship, and leaving with their own personalized ornaments to cherish.

The two spent the next hour brainstorming, Merry pulling out a hand-drawn map of the town square she'd sketched earlier. They discussed where to set up the display, how to arrange the ornaments by theme, and even the possibility of using an old oak arch to frame the exhibit.

"What if we string some lights through the arch?" Merry suggested, tapping a spot on the map where the display would go. "It would draw people's attention right to your work."

Arthur nodded approvingly. "I have some oak beams stored away. They'd make a fine frame for the display."

They talked about the logistics, Arthur considering every practical detail while Merry focused on the experience they wanted to create for the townspeople. By the time they finished, Merry felt a profound sense of satisfaction and excitement.

"Mr. Schmidt," she said, her voice full of gratitude, "I can't thank you enough. Your work is going to be the highlight of the festival, I just know it."

Arthur looked at her, surprised by her sincerity. "You give me too much credit, Miss North," he said. "But I'm grateful you think so."

## A Very Krampus Christmas

Merry shook her head, her determination unwavering. "Not at all. People deserve to know about your craftsmanship. We'll even put a special section in the festival program just for you and your ornaments."

Arthur seemed moved by her words, though he tried to hide it with a modest smile. "That's very generous of you, Merry."

She smiled back, feeling a warmth settle in her chest. "Just keep making your beautiful ornaments. They're going to bring so much joy to everyone this Christmas."

As Arthur locked up his workshop, the two shared a moment of quiet understanding, a partnership born out of mutual respect and a shared love for the town's traditions. Merry left, her heart light with anticipation. The festival was shaping up to be something truly special—perhaps even the beginning of new traditions for Tannenbaum Falls.

As she walked home, Merry's thoughts wandered back to Arthur's workshop and the meaningful connection she felt there. She couldn't wait to bring their ideas to life, certain this year's celebration would capture the spirit of the town in ways that would leave a lasting impact.

## Chapter 6

The crisp winter air bit at Merry's cheeks as she hurried down Main Street, her boots crunching through the fresh layer of snow. Ahead, the town square's towering Christmas tree gleamed under the soft glow of holiday lights, and there stood Klaus, waiting by the tree's edge, looking as handsome and mysterious as ever in his dark wool coat.

"Klaus!" Merry called, waving enthusiastically as she approached. "Hope I didn't keep you waiting long."

Klaus turned toward her, offering a rare smile that brightened his usually serious features. "Not at all, Merry. I've been admiring the town's spirit. It seems Tannenbaum Falls truly comes alive this time of year."

"Oh, you have no idea," Merry replied, looping her arm through his. "Wait until you see everything up close. There's so much magic here." She led him along the snow-dusted sidewalk, soaking in the festive garlands, the twinkling lights adorning each storefront, and the hum of Christmas carols floating on the air.

"It's like stepping into a snow globe," she sighed contentedly. "Don't you think?"

Klaus nodded, his voice carrying a touch of nostalgia. "It reminds me of Christmases long past, when people truly embraced the magic of the season."

Merry tilted her head, curious. Sometimes Klaus spoke as if he'd lived through centuries, his words full of an old-world charm that intrigued her. But tonight, she let it pass, instead offering, "Let me show you my favorite spots in town. You'll see what makes Tannenbaum Falls so special."

They wandered together, Merry pointing out the details she adored: the wreaths of holly and pinecones adorning each lamppost, the frosted shop windows showcasing whimsical holiday scenes, and the warm glow spilling from every door they passed.

As they paused in front of a little bakery, the rich aroma of cinnamon and vanilla wafted out, pulling Merry's attention to the snowflake-frosted windows. "Oh, Klaus, we have to stop here," she exclaimed, already heading toward the door. "I can almost taste the gingerbread!"

Klaus chuckled and followed her inside. "Far be it from me to stand between a baker and her treats," he said with a teasing grin.

Inside, the cozy shop enveloped them in warmth, filled with the soft chatter of patrons and the faint hum of holiday music. Merry's gaze swept the display cases lined with star-shaped sugar cookies dusted in edible glitter, gingerbread men with tiny smiles, and warm pastries fresh from the oven.

"It's like Santa's kitchen," she murmured, admiring a tray of intricately decorated cookies. "Two of those, please," she told the smiling clerk.

They found a small table by the window, and Merry took a delicate bite of her cookie, savoring the sweetness. "Mmm," she sighed. "This reminds me of the cookies my grandmother used to make for our tree-trimming parties. Do you have any holiday traditions like that?"

Klaus nodded thoughtfully, a gentle smile on his lips. "There was a time we would roast chestnuts by the fire and make hot cocoa from scratch. Simple things, but they warmed the heart."

Merry leaned in, touched by his nostalgia. "Those sound wonderful. Maybe we could bring back some of those traditions for the festival."

Klaus seemed to consider her words as they finished their treats, a comfortable silence between them as they watched the snowfall outside. When they finally stepped back into the chilly evening air, Merry felt a sense of connection to Klaus she hadn't expected.

"Oh, look at that!" Merry gasped suddenly, tugging him toward a quaint bookstore across the street. Its window displayed a tiny winter village scene, complete with miniature skaters on a frozen pond and a dusting of fake snow. "Isn't it charming?" she said, already pulling him along. "Please, let's go inside."

They entered, greeted by the comforting scent of old books and worn leather. Merry's eyes sparkled as she took in the rows upon rows of shelves, each one a new adventure waiting to be explored. "I could spend hours here," she whispered, running her fingers along a shelf. "Do you enjoy reading?"

"Very much," Klaus replied. "There's something timeless about books. They carry wisdom and wonder that we sometimes lose in the rush of life."

They browsed together, Merry's heart swelling at the thought of sharing one of her favorite pastimes with him. She had always been a hopeless romantic, and tonight felt like something out of her daydreams.

Back on the street, they continued their stroll, pausing occasionally to admire the shop displays and exchange stories of holidays past. As they reached a small boutique nestled between two larger stores, Merry's attention was immediately drawn to the array of handcrafted ornaments and unique gifts in the window.

"Oh, Klaus! Look at that adorable shop!" she exclaimed, pressing her hand against the glass. "Shall we take a peek inside?"

Klaus nodded, his smile gentle as he held the door for her. "After you, Merry."

Inside, they were greeted by rows of delicate ornaments hanging from rustic beams, each one catching the soft light and casting tiny rainbows on the walls. Merry's breath caught as she carefully lifted a hand-painted glass bauble, tracing its intricate snowflake design with her fingers.

"These are exquisite," she murmured, turning the ornament in her hand. "Can you imagine how beautiful they'd look on a Christmas tree?"

Klaus watched her, his voice warm. "Indeed. Though I'd say the joy on your face right now outshines them all."

Merry felt her cheeks warm, and she laughed, swatting his arm playfully. "Oh, you," she said. "But really—if we were decorating a tree, which one do you think would suit it best? This wooden reindeer or the glittery pinecone?"

Klaus stroked his chin thoughtfully. "While the reindeer has a certain rustic charm, I think the pinecone would catch the light beautifully."

Their conversation drifted into imagining a tree adorned with all their favorite finds, and Merry found herself lost in a daydream of cozy evenings spent decorating by a crackling fire. She quickly pushed the thought aside, reminding herself that this was about the festival—nothing more.

As they continued walking, Merry's eyes sparkled with excitement. "Let's take a detour to the town square. I want to show you the Christmas tree—it's truly magnificent."

Klaus chuckled softly, allowing himself to be led. "I've seen quite a few trees in my time, but I'm sure this one will be special."

They rounded the corner, and there it stood: a towering evergreen, draped in colorful ornaments and glowing with thousands of lights. Klaus paused beside her, both of them admiring the tree's beauty in the quiet of the snow-dusted square.

"Every year, the whole town comes together to decorate it," Merry said proudly. "See that silver star near the top? I made that in elementary school."

They slowly circled the tree, Merry pointing out various ornaments, each with its own story. As they reached the far side, a familiar sound caught her attention—an echo of gentle scraping and rhythmic tapping from a small, nearby building.

"Do you hear that?" she asked, her face lighting up. "That's Arthur at his workshop. Want to go see?"

Without waiting for an answer, she led him down a narrow side street. The sound grew louder as they approached a quaint, stone-fronted workshop with a steady curl of smoke from the chimney. Merry pushed open the door, letting the warm, earthy scent of pine and sawdust wash over them.

"Arthur!" she called, spotting him bent over his workbench, carefully shaping a wooden reindeer with practiced hands. "Look who I brought to see your workshop!"

Arthur looked up, his face brightening as he spotted them. "Well, if it isn't Merry North and her friend," he said with a welcoming nod. "Come in, come in. Let me show you what I'm working on."

They stepped closer, captivated by the tiny details Arthur had carved into the reindeer. Klaus let out a low murmur of appreciation. "It's incredible. The detail is… exquisite."

Merry grinned, unable to tear her gaze from the little wooden figure. "Arthur, you make them look so lifelike. How do you do it?"

Arthur chuckled, setting down his chisel. "It's all about patience and love. Each piece has its own story, and I'm just here to help bring it out."

As Arthur shared more about his process, Merry felt a deep sense of admiration for the man who had spent years honing his craft. She turned to Klaus, noticing how intently he was listening, seeming to absorb every word.

"The festival's going to be magical with your creations, Arthur," Merry said with a grin. "I can't wait to see everything displayed."

Arthur gave them both an appreciative nod. "It's you two who've brought this old workshop back to life. I hadn't felt this inspired in years."

Merry's heart swelled with gratitude. This was why she'd come back to Tannenbaum Falls: to find this warmth, this sense of belonging. It was what made the town—and the people in it—so special.

As she and Klaus stepped out into the evening once more, Merry clutched a small wooden ornament Arthur had given her, its smooth surface cool against her palm. She took a breath, savoring the feeling of the snow falling softly around them.

"I never expected to feel so at home here," she said quietly, glancing at Klaus. "But somehow, it feels right."

Klaus gave her hand a gentle squeeze, a warmth in his touch that seemed to melt away the winter chill. "There's something about Tannenbaum Falls," he replied, his voice steady and warm. "It's as if the spirit of Christmas has found its home here."

They walked in comfortable silence, the snowflakes swirling around them in the soft glow of the streetlights. As they passed a brightly lit shop window, Merry's laughter bubbled up, light and joyful. "Oh, look at that!" she said, pointing to a display of animatronic elves dressed in festive red and green, dancing and spinning with little mechanical grins.

Klaus chuckled, the sound warm and genuine. "They do seem to enjoy themselves," he observed with a smirk. Merry leaned into him, sharing the laugh and relishing the closeness between them.

They strolled through the quiet, snow-covered streets, taking in the twinkling lights and soft hum of holiday music that floated through the air from hidden speakers along the lampposts. Merry felt an overwhelming sense of peace settle over her as they reached the square's edge.

## A Very Krampus Christmas

"I feel like I could stay here forever," she murmured, letting out a contented sigh as they paused to gaze back at the tree, which stood like a sentinel in the square, spreading its light over the sleeping town.

Klaus turned toward her, his tone gentle. "Some places just have a way of making us feel like we've found what we were looking for, even if we didn't know we were searching."

His words lingered in the air, and Merry found herself holding onto the quiet, tender moment, feeling as if Tannenbaum Falls itself had wrapped them in its warmth.

"Klaus," she said softly, almost hesitating. "I know we haven't known each other long, but it feels like... I don't know, like you've always been here."

Klaus's gaze softened. "Funny," he replied, his voice just above a whisper. "I was thinking the same about you."

They shared a smile, and for that one peaceful moment, everything felt perfectly in place.

## Chapter 7

Snowflakes swirled outside the frost-covered window of Tannenbaum Falls' community center as Merry North's voice cut through the room with urgent concern.

"Klaus, we can't hold the festival in these conditions! It's not safe," Merry insisted, gesturing to the blizzard raging beyond the glass. "People could end up stranded, or worse."

Klaus Krampus stood across from her, arms folded, his expression unwavering. "The Winter Wonderland Festival has never been canceled in 150 years, Merry. Surely we can find a way to preserve the tradition."

Merry sighed, her breath visible in the chilly air. She knew how much Klaus valued tradition—it was one of the things that had drawn her to him. But this was different.

"I know how much it means to everyone," she said, laying a hand on his arm. "My grandmother's cookie recipes have been part of this festival for decades. But people's safety has to come first."

Klaus's stance softened a bit at her touch. "Maybe if we moved some activities indoors…" he mused.

Merry shook her head, her auburn curls bouncing. "The community center's already full of vendor booths. And what about the sledding hill? The ice sculpture garden? We can't just…"

A particularly strong gust of wind rattled the windows, and Merry pulled her cardigan tighter around her shoulders. Klaus noticed her shiver and stepped closer, his presence warm and reassuring.

"You're right to be concerned," he admitted. "But postponing could be disastrous for local businesses that have been preparing all year. We need a compromise."

Merry's mind raced, trying to envision a solution, but images of cars skidding on icy roads and children lost in snowdrifts haunted her thoughts. "I just keep thinking of Mrs. Clausen trying to navigate her walker through snowdrifts," she murmured. "Or little Timmy Johnson getting separated from his parents in a white-out. Klaus, I couldn't forgive myself if something happened."

Klaus looked at her thoughtfully. "Your compassion does you credit," he said gently. "Perhaps we could discuss this further over some hot cocoa? I think I might have a few ideas that could work."

Grateful for the pause, Merry nodded. Together, they walked toward the small kitchenette, and for the first time that day, she felt a glimmer of hope. If anyone could find a solution that honored tradition and kept everyone safe, it was Klaus.

Klaus handed her a steaming mug of cocoa, the rich aroma filling the cozy office space. He took a sip, his expression pensive.

"Merry, I understand your concerns," he began, his voice carrying a calm, steady confidence. "But this festival isn't just about lights and gingerbread. It's about bringing people together. For many, it's the one time they feel the magic of community."

Merry wrapped her hands around the warm mug, feeling some of her tension ease. "I know, Klaus. But—"

"Think of young Sally Peterson," Klaus continued, his tone softening. "This is her first Christmas without her father. The festival might be just what she needs to feel joy again."

Merry's heart clenched at the thought. She'd seen Sally around town, her face clouded by grief. Imagining the little girl's smile as she marveled at the festival lights brought a lump to Merry's throat.

"You're right," she admitted quietly. "But how can we make it safe?"

Klaus's mouth curved in a small smile. "That's where creativity comes in. Let's brainstorm some ideas, shall we?"

Just then, the door creaked open, and Arthur Schmidt shuffled in, brushing snow from his shoulders. He glanced at the two of them, his face lighting up with a knowing smile.

"Ah, just the two I was hoping to find," Arthur greeted. "I couldn't help but overhear. How about setting up heated tents and serving hot drinks to keep everyone warm?"

Merry felt a spark of excitement at his suggestion. "Arthur, that's brilliant! Tents would keep people out of the snow, and warm drinks would add to the coziness."

Klaus rubbed his chin thoughtfully. "It's an intriguing idea. The tents could provide shelter, and hot cocoa or cider could keep everyone's spirits high."

Merry nodded eagerly, picturing the layout. "We could set up the tents around the town square, transforming it into a cozy winter haven."

"But the cost…" Klaus's tone turned practical. "Heated tents and enough hot drinks for the town aren't cheap."

Merry's excitement dimmed as she considered the expense. "You're right. It would put a serious dent in our budget."

Klaus leaned back, his gaze thoughtful. "We could make cuts elsewhere. Maybe scale back on the decorations?"

"No," Merry interjected quickly, shaking her head. "The decorations make it magical. There has to be another way."

She bit her lip, an idea forming. "What if… what if we postponed the festival? Just for a week or two, until the weather improves?"

Klaus's eyebrows raised in surprise. "Postpone? But, Merry, the festival has always been held on the same date. It's part of our town's tradition."

Merry exhaled, running a hand through her hair. "I know, but sometimes traditions need to adapt. Isn't it better to have a safe, joyful festival a little later than risk anyone's well-being?"

Merry leaned forward, hands clasped on the table. "Klaus, I get it. Tradition is important. But our first responsibility is to the community's safety."

Klaus's brow furrowed, his voice steady. "The festival isn't just about tradition, Merry. It's about bringing light to the darkest part of the year, rekindling hope when it's needed most."

The warmth of the cocoa and the cozy ambiance of the room intensified their debate. Merry breathed in the lingering scent of cinnamon and nutmeg, memories of past festivals filling her heart.

"I agree," she said softly. "But what's the use of hope if people can't make it to the festival? Those roads could be treacherous."

Klaus acknowledged her point with a nod. "True, but canceling or postponing could deflate the town's spirit. For some, this festival is the highlight of the year."

Merry paused, searching for a middle ground. "What if we did both?" she proposed, her voice lifting with newfound energy. "We keep the indoor events as planned—the cookie exchange, the toymaking workshop, the caroling contest. And we postpone the outdoor activities—the sleigh rides, the ice sculpture competition, the bonfire—until the weather clears."

Klaus tilted his head, considering her suggestion. "A hybrid approach?" he murmured, rubbing his chin thoughtfully. "It could maintain the tradition while addressing safety."

"Exactly!" Merry said, her enthusiasm rekindling. "We'd still keep the original festival date, but extend the celebration a little longer. It could even become a new tradition—Tannenbaum Falls' Winter Festival Fortnight!"

A slow smile crept across Klaus's face. "You may be onto something, Merry North. It's not a perfect solution, but it's a compromise that could work for everyone."

Together, Merry and Klaus huddled over the revised festival schedule, spread out across the bakery's wooden table. The aroma of fresh pastries filled the room as they marked which events would stay and which ones would be rescheduled.

"All right," Merry said, tapping the paper. "We need to decide what stays indoors."

Klaus nodded, leaning in with concentration. "The cookie exchange can stay. It's always been indoors anyway."

Merry grinned. "And your toymaking workshop. The kids would be devastated if that got postponed."

"Agreed," Klaus replied with a rare hint of warmth in his tone. "But how do we get the word out without causing confusion?"

Merry considered it, a finger tapping her chin. "We could put up notices around town, maybe even go door-to-door if we have to. And social media, of course. Arthur's daughter could help spread the word online."

As if summoned, the bell above the bakery door chimed, and the festival planning team entered, brushing snow off their coats. Merry felt a surge of affection for these dedicated volunteers.

"Everyone," she called out, gathering their attention, "we've got some changes to discuss."

As she and Klaus outlined their hybrid plan, the team responded with enthusiasm, undeterred by the adjustments.

"Ooh, what if we set up a hot cocoa bar for the indoor events?" suggested Emily, the town librarian. "With different toppings and flavors?"

Arthur chimed in with a grin. "And we could have an indoor snowman-building contest—with cotton balls and craft supplies!"

Merry's heart filled with pride as the ideas flowed. This was the spirit of Tannenbaum Falls—creative, resilient, and always willing to work together. She exchanged a glance with Klaus, a sense of accomplishment settling between them.

As the team left, Merry leaned back, watching Klaus review the finalized event schedule with a rare look of satisfaction.

"You know," she said quietly, "I think we managed to strike a pretty good balance."

Klaus looked up, meeting her gaze. "Indeed," he replied, his tone carrying a hint of warmth that made her heart flutter. "You've shown a great deal of flexibility while still honoring tradition. It's admirable."

Merry blushed, tucking a stray curl behind her ear. "Well, I couldn't have done it without you. Your dedication reminded me why these traditions matter so much to everyone."

They shared a quiet moment, the comfortable silence filled with a newfound camaraderie. Merry marveled at how well they worked

## Chapter 8

Merry's boots crunched through the deepening snow as she and Klaus made their way down Main Street, the wind whipping her auburn hair across her face. Tannenbaum Falls had transformed into a winter wonderland, but Merry's only focus was reaching her grandmother's bakery.

"Just a little farther!" she called over her shoulder, breath forming mist in the icy air. Klaus's tall figure kept steady behind her through the swirling flakes.

"Right behind you," he called back, his voice deep and reassuring even against the howling wind.

Merry's heart pounded, both from the urgency of their mission and a nagging worry. The annual Christmas cookie festival was just hours away, and hundreds of cookies still needed baking. The entire town was counting on her to uphold the tradition her grandmother had started—and she couldn't let them down.

Finally, the bakery's familiar red awning appeared. Merry fumbled with her keys, hands numb from the cold. "Come on, come on," she muttered, trying to slot the key into the lock.

Klaus stepped beside her and gently took the keys. "Allow me," he offered, easily turning the lock and pushing open the door.

They hurried inside, but Merry's relief faded quickly; the bakery was shrouded in darkness.

"Oh no," she whispered. "The power's out."

Klaus moved to the light switch, flipping it a few times, though the room remained dark. "It seems the storm's knocked out the electricity," he observed, calm as ever despite the predicament.

Merry's mind raced. The town depended on these cookies; this festival was a highlight of the season. She could almost hear her grandmother's words: "Where there's a will, there's a way, my little sugarplum."

"We can't give up," she said firmly, more to herself than to Klaus. "There has to be a solution."

Klaus nodded, his face steady and resolved in the dim light filtering through the frosted windows. "Indeed. If we put our heads together, perhaps we'll find a way."

Taking a deep breath, Merry inhaled the comforting scent of cinnamon and vanilla that still lingered in the bakery. It brought back memories of countless hours spent here with her grandmother, learning family recipes.

"Alright," she said, squaring her shoulders. "Let's get creative. We have all the ingredients; we just need a way to bake them."

As they stood in the darkened bakery, surrounded by the cold, silent ovens, Merry felt a spark of hope. With Klaus by her side, there was nothing they couldn't overcome. After all, Christmas was about more than just tradition; it was about finding joy even in challenges.

A thought struck Merry. "The wood-burning oven!" She pointed to the corner of the bakery. "Grandma always said it made the best cookies. We can use that!"

Klaus's brows lifted, a smile tugging at the corner of his mouth. "A brilliant idea, Merry. I'm impressed."

They set to work gathering firewood from the storage shed behind the bakery. As they stacked the logs into the oven, Merry's fingers brushed against Klaus's, sending a warmth through her despite the cold air.

"You know," Merry began, trying to ignore the flutter in her stomach, "I've never actually used this oven before. Grandma swore by it, but I always stuck to the electric ones."

Klaus chuckled, his voice rumbling in the quiet space. "Then we'll learn together. Although, I must confess, my baking skills are quite… elementary."

Merry giggled, "The great Toymaker, humbled by a batch of cookies? I never thought I'd see the day."

"Ah," Klaus replied, amusement in his tone, "toys and treats are different beasts. But both bring joy to children's hearts."

## A Very Krampus Christmas

While they waited for the oven to heat, Merry leaned against the counter, a mischievous grin spreading across her face. "Alright, Klaus—what's your worst baking disaster?"

Klaus rubbed his chin thoughtfully. "Once, I tried making gingerbread men for the elves. Let's just say the shapes were more... abstract than edible."

Merry burst into laughter, imagining the scene. "Oh, I can relate. My first attempt at Grandma's sugar cookies ended up as one giant, lumpy blob. Dad called it the 'Cookie Monster.'"

As they swapped stories of baking mishaps, Merry felt the tension of the evening begin to melt away. There was something so natural about working with Klaus, as if they'd known each other for years.

Merry glanced out the frosted window, watching snowflakes dance in the dim light of the street lamps outside. The warmth from the old wood-burning oven wrapped around her like a cozy blanket, a welcome contrast to the winter chill beyond.

"You know," she started, turning to Klaus with a gentle smile, "I never expected to fall in love with a place like Tannenbaum Falls. But there's something... magical about this town, especially at Christmas."

Klaus nodded. "Indeed. It's as if time pauses here, preserving the true spirit of the holidays."

Merry's heart warmed at his words. "That's why I'm so determined to keep my grandmother's bakery going. It's more than just cookies—it's about holding on to those traditions."

"A noble pursuit," Klaus replied, his voice thoughtful. "Traditions can be fragile. It's good you're preserving them."

Merry tilted her head, catching his phrasing. "You talk like you've lived through centuries of Christmases," she teased.

Klaus chuckled softly. "Perhaps I have an old soul. Now, tell me, what's your favorite tradition here in Tannenbaum Falls?"

As Merry launched into a story about the annual tree lighting ceremony, a warm connection seemed to deepen between them. She shared her fondest memories, realizing how much she wanted him to understand the town she loved.

A delicious aroma filled the room, interrupting her thoughts. "The cookies!" Merry exclaimed, rushing to the oven. They carefully removed the trays, revealing golden-brown cookies, perfectly baked.

"We did it!" Merry's smile brightened as she took in the sight.

Klaus returned her smile, pride in his expression. "Indeed. Now, let's get them boxed up before they cool."

They fell into an easy rhythm, working side by side to package the cookies, and Merry couldn't help but marvel at how in sync their movements were, as if they'd been baking together for years. This feels right, she thought. Like they were meant to be here, saving Christmas together.

The wind howled outside as Merry peered through the bakery's frosted window. "Ready to brave the storm?" she asked, pulling on her mittens.

Klaus nodded, his voice full of resolve. "For Tannenbaum Falls' Christmas spirit? Always."

They stepped out into the swirling snow, each balancing stacks of cookie boxes. Merry's boots crunched through the fresh powder as she navigated the slippery sidewalk.

"Careful," Klaus warned, his hand instinctively steadying her elbow. "These streets are treacherous tonight."

Merry felt a warmth bloom in her chest. "My hero," she laughed, just as she slipped on a patch of ice.

Klaus caught her quickly, keeping the cookie boxes miraculously upright. "You were saying?" he teased, a rare grin spreading across his face.

As they continued through the winter wonderland, Merry found herself stealing glances at him. There was something comforting and familiar about Klaus, like a cherished Christmas ornament rediscovered every year.

"Tell me, Klaus," she asked, her breath visible in the frosty air, "have you seen a storm quite like this?"

He glanced up, surveying the swirling snowflakes with a hint of nostalgia. "A few, perhaps. But each snowfall has its own kind of magic, don't you think?"

Merry nodded. "It's like a fresh start for the town, everything blanketed in white."

They rounded the corner, and the festival venue came into view. Volunteers struggled against the wind, tinsel and lights tangled in their hands.

"Oh dear," Merry said, surveying the scene. "Looks like we have our work cut out for us."

Klaus squared his shoulders, determination settling on his face. "Then let's get to it."

Merry and Klaus stood side by side, surveying the now-transformed festival grounds. Lights draped over snow-laden evergreens, and ornaments hung from every surface, casting a magical glow over the square.

"It's perfect," Merry whispered, taking it all in. She turned to Klaus with a satisfied smile. "We did it."

Klaus nodded, a softness to his expression. "Your grandmother would be proud, Merry."

A lump formed in her throat at the thought. "Thank you," she said, voice thick with emotion.

They shared a quiet moment of pride before the distant chime of the clock tower reminded them of their task.

"Oh!" Merry exclaimed. "The festival opens in thirty minutes!"

Klaus nodded. "We'd best check on everything. Shall we divide and conquer?"

Merry shook her head, feeling a surprising reluctance to part ways. "Let's tackle it together. Two heads are better than one, right?"

They moved through the venue side by side, going over each station. Every now and then, Merry felt Klaus's reassuring presence beside her, grounding her amidst the hustle.

Finally, the doors opened, and a wave of townspeople poured into the festival. The aroma of her grandmother's gingerbread filled the hall, and Merry took her place at the cookie stand, catching glimpses of Klaus, who worked skillfully at the toy-making area, carving wooden figures for delighted children.

As the night went on, Merry found herself drifting over to Klaus whenever she had a free moment, exchanging brief, meaningful words and knowing smiles that left her heart fluttering. Each time she returned to her cookie station, she felt more certain of the connection growing between them.

"How are the toys coming along?" she asked during a lull, leaning close enough to hear him over the bustling crowd.

Klaus looked up from his work, a hint of pride in his expression. "Splendidly. And your cookies seem to be the highlight of the evening."

Merry laughed softly. "We make quite the team, don't we?"

As they worked through the evening, Merry noticed how naturally they fell into step, almost as if they'd been sharing these responsibilities for years. She caught herself watching him as he interacted with the townspeople, his warmth and quiet strength making her feel as if they were part of something even greater than a festival. Her grandmother would have loved him, she thought, with a pang of nostalgia.

As the night wore on, the crowd began to thin, leaving Merry and Klaus with a few volunteers to clean up. Together, they tidied the hall, gathering decorations and packing away leftover supplies, working in sync as they folded up tables and swept the floors. It felt right, this quiet rhythm they shared amidst the soft glow of the remaining Christmas lights.

As they neared the end of their tasks, Merry glanced at Klaus, a feeling of reluctance tugging at her. "I suppose this is where we part ways," she said, though she felt her heart sink at the thought.

Klaus hesitated, his gaze warm as he met hers. "Does it have to be?" His voice was low and inviting.

Merry's heart skipped a beat. "What do you mean?"

Klaus stepped closer, his hand brushing lightly against hers. "I find myself... not wanting this night to end," he admitted, his tone filled with sincerity. "Perhaps we could spend a little more time together? Maybe explore this connection?"

Her heart raced, and a soft smile spread across her face as she intertwined her fingers with his. "I'd like that very much, Klaus."

They stepped outside into the peaceful quiet of the snow-covered town. Flakes drifted softly down, and the lights from the street lamps cast a warm glow over the empty streets. Klaus offered her his arm, and Merry took it, leaning into his warmth as they strolled through the enchanting winter landscape.

"You know," Merry began, breaking the comfortable silence, "when I first came back to Tannenbaum Falls, I didn't imagine I'd find... this."

Klaus glanced down at her, curiosity lighting his expression. "And what is 'this' exactly?"

Merry stopped walking, turning to face him. "A sense of belonging. A community that feels like family." She hesitated, her voice soft. "And... you."

## A Very Krampus Christmas

Klaus looked at her, surprise and hope mingling in his expression. For a moment, she feared she'd said too much, but then he reached up, brushing a stray snowflake from her hair with a tenderness that made her breath hitch.

"Merry," he said quietly, "you've brought more joy to this town—and to me—than you realize."

Merry felt herself drawn closer to him, her gaze drifting to his lips before meeting his again. Slowly, Klaus leaned in, giving her time to pull away, but Merry moved to meet him halfway. Their lips met in a soft, tender kiss, as the world around them seemed to fall away, leaving only the two of them in a bubble of warmth and wonder.

As they pulled apart, both slightly breathless, Merry's face broke into a radiant smile. "I think," she murmured, "that this is the beginning of something truly wonderful."

Klaus mirrored her smile, his arm wrapping around her as the snow continued to fall around them, blanketing Tannenbaum Falls in the magic of their new beginning.

## Chapter 9

Merry's boots crunched through the snow as she and Klaus hurried down Main Street, the icy wind whipping her auburn hair around her face. Tannenbaum Falls had transformed into a winter wonderland, but Merry's only focus was reaching her grandmother's bakery.

"Just a little farther!" she called over her shoulder, her breath misting in the frigid air. Klaus's tall frame was a shadowy outline through the whirling flakes behind her.

"Right behind you," he called back, his deep voice cutting through the gusts of wind with reassurance.

Merry's heart raced, driven by both the urgency of their task and a rising worry. The annual Christmas cookie festival was just hours away, and they still had hundreds of cookies to bake. The thought of letting down the town—and failing to honor her grandmother's legacy—pressed heavily on her.

At last, the warm glow of the bakery's red awning came into view. Merry fumbled with her keys, her fingers numb from the cold. "Come on, come on," she muttered, trying to slip the key into the lock.

Klaus appeared beside her, gently taking the keys. "Allow me," he said, smoothly unlocking the door.

As they stumbled inside, Merry's relief was brief; the bakery lay in darkness.

"Oh no," she murmured, feeling her heart sink. "The power's out."

Klaus moved to the light switch, flicking it a few times without luck. "The storm must have knocked out the electricity," he observed, his voice calm despite the situation.

Merry's mind spun. How could they bake without power? The entire town depended on these cookies, and her grandmother's words echoed in her memory: "Where there's a will, there's a way, my little sugarplum."

"We can't give up," Merry said firmly, as much to herself as to Klaus. "There has to be a solution."

Klaus nodded, determination glinting in his expression. "Indeed. If we put our heads together, we'll find a way."

Taking a deep breath, Merry took in the comforting scent of cinnamon and vanilla that lingered in the air—a reminder of the countless hours she'd spent here with her grandmother. It grounded her, and she felt a spark of hope reignite.

"Alright," she said, squaring her shoulders. "We have all the ingredients. We just need to get creative about baking them."

As they stood together in the quiet, darkened bakery, Merry felt a sense of reassurance settle over her. With Klaus by her side, she knew they could overcome any challenge—Christmas spirit and all.

Inspiration struck, and Merry's face lit up. "The wood-burning oven!" She pointed to the back corner. "Grandma always said it made the best cookies. We can use that!"

Klaus's brows lifted with a glimmer of approval. "Brilliant idea, Merry. You're resourceful."

They sprang into action, gathering firewood from the storage shed behind the bakery. As they stacked the logs into the old oven, Merry's fingers brushed against Klaus's hand, sending a brief, warm jolt through her despite the cold.

"You know," Merry began, trying to ignore the flutter in her chest, "I've never actually used this oven before. Grandma swore by it, but I always took the electric route."

Klaus chuckled, his voice a deep rumble. "Then we'll learn together. Although, I must confess, my baking skills are fairly... basic."

Merry grinned. "The great Toymaker, daunted by a batch of cookies? Never thought I'd see the day."

"Toys and treats are different beasts," he replied with a dry smile. "Though both bring joy in their own way."

As the oven warmed, Merry leaned against the counter with a mischievous grin. "So, tell me, Klaus. What's your biggest baking disaster?"

Klaus rubbed his chin thoughtfully. "Once, I tried making gingerbread men for the elves. Let's just say they were more... abstract than edible."

Merry burst out laughing, imagining the scene. "Oh, I can relate. My first attempt at Grandma's sugar cookies ended in one lumpy blob. Dad called it the 'Cookie Monster.'"

They shared stories of baking mishaps, and soon, the tension melted away. Klaus's dry humor and quiet confidence were a balm to her nerves. For the first time that night, she thought maybe the power outage was a blessing in disguise.

Merry gazed out the frosted window, watching snowflakes drift past the dim glow of the street lamps. The warmth from the wood-burning oven filled the bakery with a cozy embrace, pushing back the winter chill.

"You know," she began, turning to Klaus with a gentle smile, "I never thought I'd fall in love with a place like Tannenbaum Falls. But there's something truly magical about this town, especially at Christmas."

Klaus nodded thoughtfully. "It's as if time slows here, capturing the spirit of the holidays."

Merry felt her heart warm at his words. "Exactly. That's why I'm so determined to keep my grandmother's bakery going. It's not just about the cookies; it's about preserving traditions."

"A worthy goal," Klaus said, his voice rich with sincerity. "I've seen how easily old ways can fade... if they're not cared for."

Merry tilted her head, intrigued by his phrasing. "You talk like you've lived through centuries of Christmases," she teased.

Klaus chuckled. "Perhaps I have an old soul. Now, tell me—what's your favorite tradition in Tannenbaum Falls?"

As Merry described the annual tree-lighting ceremony, she felt her connection with Klaus deepen. There was something about his presence that felt like stepping into a well-loved story, full of comfort and discovery.

A heavenly aroma drifted through the room, breaking her thoughts. "The cookies!" she exclaimed, hurrying to the oven.

They carefully removed the trays, revealing golden-brown cookies, perfectly baked. She and Klaus exchanged a look of pure joy and relief.

"We did it!" Merry beamed.

"Indeed," Klaus replied with a nod. "Now, let's get these packed up before they cool."

Working together in seamless rhythm, they boxed the cookies, Merry marveling at how natural it felt to be side by side with him. This, she thought, felt like more than just baking—it felt like they were part of something meaningful, something lasting.

The wind howled outside as Merry peered through the bakery's frosted window. "Ready to brave the storm?" she asked, pulling on her mittens.

Klaus adjusted his scarf and nodded. "For the sake of Tannenbaum Falls' Christmas spirit? Always."

They stepped into the swirling snow, balancing stacks of cookie boxes. Merry's boots crunched through the fresh powder as she navigated the slippery path.

"Careful now," Klaus warned, reaching to steady her as she hit a patch of ice. "These streets are treacherous tonight."

Merry laughed, warmth blooming in her chest. "My hero," she teased, just as her foot slipped again.

Klaus caught her, his grip strong and steady, saving both her and the cookies. "You were saying?" he asked with a rare grin.

As they made their way through the snowy wonderland, Merry found herself glancing at Klaus. He felt familiar, like a cherished holiday memory brought to life.

"Tell me, Klaus," she said, breath puffing in the frosty air, "have you ever seen a storm like this?"

He paused, gazing at the falling snow. "Perhaps. But each snowfall has its own beauty, don't you think?"

Merry nodded. "It's like the town is getting a fresh start, blanketed in white."

They turned a corner, and the festival venue came into view, volunteers struggling against the wind with tinsel and lights tangled in their hands.

"Oh dear," Merry murmured. "Looks like we have our work cut out for us."

Klaus squared his shoulders. "Then let's get to it."

As Merry and Klaus worked, the once-barren festival grounds transformed into a shimmering display of lights and decorations. The venue sparkled like a jewel nestled in a blanket of white.

"It's breathtaking," Merry whispered, admiring their handiwork. She turned to Klaus with a satisfied smile. "We did it."

Klaus nodded. "Your grandmother would be proud, Merry."

Emotion welled up in Merry's chest. "Thank you," she said quietly. "I hope we've honored her vision."

They shared a quiet moment before the distant chime of the clock reminded them of the task ahead.

"Oh!" Merry exclaimed, turning to face him. "The festival opens in thirty minutes!"

Klaus raised an eyebrow. "We'd better make sure everything is in place. Shall we divide and conquer?"

Merry shook her head, eager to stay close to him. "Let's do it together. Two heads are better than one."

They moved through the venue, checking each station. At each turn, Merry felt Klaus's presence beside her, his calm assurance lifting her spirits.

Finally, the doors opened, and a wave of townspeople flooded in. As Merry took her place at the cookie stand, she watched Klaus work at the toy-making area, his hands skillfully carving wooden figures for the children gathered around him.

As the evening progressed, Merry found herself drawn to him, taking every chance to share brief words and quiet smiles, their bond strengthening with each exchange.

"Merry," Klaus said during a quiet moment, his voice low and warm, "your dedication is truly inspiring."

Merry felt a warmth spread through her chest. "Oh, Klaus, I couldn't have done it without you. You've been my anchor."

He took her hand gently, his touch warm amidst the bustling crowd around them. "You've brought such light to this town, Merry. More than you know."

Merry's heart swelled, and she couldn't help but feel that something magical was unfolding between them. Their moment was briefly interrupted as a burst of laughter and cheer filled the room. She looked around at the joyful faces, families sharing cookies, children marveling at Klaus's handmade toys. Everything felt like it had fallen into place.

"It's everything I dreamed it would be," she whispered, glancing back at Klaus. "We really did it."

Klaus's expression softened, a smile tugging at his lips. "Together, yes. I couldn't have asked for a better partner."

As the night wore on, the crowd began to thin. Merry and Klaus started cleaning up the festival hall, gathering decorations and packing away supplies. They moved quietly through the space, both tired but content, surrounded by the twinkling lights and the lingering scent of pine and cinnamon.

Merry let out a soft sigh. "I suppose this is where we part ways," she said, a hint of reluctance in her voice.

Klaus stepped closer, his hand brushing lightly against hers. "Does it have to be?" His voice was warm and inviting, carrying a promise that made her heart skip a beat.

Merry looked up, a gentle smile spreading across her face. "What are you suggesting?"

He hesitated, a tenderness in his expression. "I find myself... not wanting this night to end. Perhaps we could continue getting to know each other, maybe even start a new tradition of our own?"

Her smile grew, and she intertwined her fingers with his, savoring the warmth of his touch. "I'd like that very much, Klaus."

They stepped outside into the quiet beauty of the snow-covered town. Soft snowflakes drifted down around them, settling on Merry's auburn hair as she pulled her coat tighter. Klaus offered his arm, and she took it, feeling a pleasant warmth as they strolled down the peaceful streets.

"You know," Merry began, breaking the comfortable silence, "when I first came back to Tannenbaum Falls, I never imagined I'd find... this."

Klaus looked down at her, a curious smile forming. "And what is 'this,' exactly?"

Merry stopped walking, turning to face him fully. "A sense of home. Belonging. And... you."

Klaus's gaze softened, and for a moment, he simply took in her words. Finally, he reached out, brushing a stray snowflake from her hair with a gentle touch that made her heart race.

"Merry," he said quietly, his voice filled with warmth, "you've brought more joy to my life—and to this town—than I ever expected."

Feeling her heart lift, Merry stepped closer. Their faces were just inches apart, and in that quiet moment, it felt as if the whole world had fallen away, leaving only the two of them.

Slowly, Klaus leaned in, giving her every chance to pull back. But she met him halfway, and their lips met in a soft, lingering kiss. The snow fell softly around them, wrapping them in a cocoon of warmth and magic.

As they pulled back, both slightly breathless, Merry couldn't hold back a smile. "I think," she said softly, "that this is the beginning of something wonderful."

Klaus nodded, his expression tender. "I couldn't agree more."

They walked arm in arm through the quiet streets, sharing a newfound closeness, the snow continuing to fall around them as a silent witness to their promising future together.

# Chapter 10

The bakery bell's chime faded, leaving Merry alone in the cozy warmth of Millie's. The scent of cinnamon and vanilla filled the air, a comforting reminder of her grandmother's presence. She sipped her hot cocoa, gazing out the frosted window at the lights of Tannenbaum Falls, a place that had become unexpectedly dear to her.

"Oh, Millie," she murmured. "What am I going to do?"

She thought of Klaus, his warm humor, and the spark he brought into her life. A small smile appeared as she recalled how he had insisted on trying every type of cookie in the bakery. He'd grinned and claimed he was "catching up on missed cookie experiences."

Merry let her fingers trace the worn wood of the bakery counter. Her grandmother's legacy was all around her, but the weight of it felt heavier today. She had questions about the future—about herself.

"Is this truly my passion?" she wondered, looking at the shelves of cookie jars and recipe books. "Or am I just following in Gram's footsteps because it's expected?"

The bakery had always been a safe haven, but now, it felt both comforting and confining. She reached for a cookie, chewing thoughtfully as she mulled over the past months. For the first time, she questioned if she was missing something—if there was more to explore outside these familiar walls.

Needing to clear her mind, Merry grabbed her coat from the hook and stepped into the brisk evening. Snow crunched beneath her boots as she walked down the sidewalk, pulling her scarf tighter against the cold. The lights of Tannenbaum Falls glowed all around her, festive and inviting. A smile crept onto her face as the town's Christmas tree came into view, its lights casting a warm glow over the square.

"This town is magical," she said softly, her voice blending with the quiet of the winter night. "But is magic enough?"

Merry wandered down Main Street, her steps slowing as she reached Tinsel's Toy Shop. The windows were decorated with whimsical scenes of trains and toys, and she caught her reflection in the frosty glass, looking back at herself with a mixture of curiosity and contentment.

The door to the shop swung open, and Mrs. Tinsel bustled out, her arms full of garlands. "Merry! Just the person I need. Can you give me a hand with these decorations?"

Merry smiled, reaching out to help. "Of course, Mrs. Tinsel."

They worked together, stringing garlands across the storefront as townsfolk bustled around them, preparing for the festival. The sense of community surrounded her, and as she tied off a bow, she felt a wave of warmth settle over her.

"It's amazing how everyone comes together like this," she remarked.

Mrs. Tinsel nodded, her face glowing. "That's Tannenbaum Falls for you. We're more than just a town—we're family."

The words struck a chord, filling Merry with a deep sense of belonging. "I've never felt anything quite like it," she admitted, her voice catching.

Mrs. Tinsel patted her arm. "You're part of this family now. We're so glad you're here."

After finishing, Merry continued her walk with a lighter heart, her thoughts drifting from her uncertainties to the town and people she'd grown to love.

Finding a quiet bench in the town park, Merry settled onto it, watching snowflakes drift lazily in the light of a streetlamp. She held out her hand, catching a delicate flake and watching it melt against her skin. A sense of peace washed over her as she watched the snow, each flake unique, coming together to create a beautiful whole.

She closed her eyes, allowing the stillness of the moment to settle around her. Slowly, she realized that her doubts were like these snowflakes—fleeting and part of a larger picture she hadn't yet pieced together.

A burst of laughter brought Merry back to the present. She opened her eyes to see a group of children nearby, their cheeks pink from the cold as they rolled large snowballs across the park.

"Come on, Timmy! We need to make the middle part bigger!" a little girl called out.

Merry smiled as she watched their playful teamwork. Their joy was infectious, a reminder of the simple magic of the season.

"They're having the time of their lives with just snow and imagination," she murmured, her own worries fading as she watched.

Her thoughts drifted to Klaus. She felt a warmth in her chest, an affection she hadn't known she was capable of feeling. He was kind, wise, and as mysterious as the winter night.

"Oh, Klaus," she whispered to herself. "What am I going to do about you?"

The children's laughter rang out again, and Merry found herself envious of their uncomplicated happiness. Maybe that's what love should be, she thought—simple, joyful, something you create together.

But doubts soon crept back in. "What if I'm not enough for him? And the bakery... can I really balance both?"

Her fingers traced patterns in the snow beside her as she mulled over her thoughts. The answers she sought seemed as elusive as the snowflakes dancing around her.

A buzz in her pocket interrupted her thoughts. Fumbling with her mittens, she managed to pull out her phone. Her heart skipped a beat when she saw Klaus's name on the screen.

"Speak of the devil," she murmured, her voice tinged with anticipation.

The message read: *"Merry, I hope I'm not disturbing you. Could we talk? Would you meet me in the town square?"*

Merry's breath caught. She re-read the message, her fingers hovering over the screen as a thrill ran through her.

She typed back quickly: *"Of course, Klaus. I'll be there in a few minutes."*

Standing up, she brushed snow from her coat and took a deep breath, letting a whirlwind of emotions wash over her—hope, curiosity, and excitement all battling for space in her heart.

With every step toward the town square, Merry's heart beat faster. She glanced around at the lights as she approached the square, the twinkling glow surrounding the giant Christmas tree at its center.

"Will this conversation bring clarity," she wondered aloud, "or just add more questions?"

Taking one last deep breath, she squared her shoulders and stepped forward.

Merry spotted Klaus near the tree, his figure silhouetted against the festive lights. As she approached, he smiled warmly.

"Merry," he greeted, his voice gentle. "Thank you for coming."

"Of course," she replied, tucking a strand of hair behind her ear. "I'm glad you reached out."

Klaus gestured to a nearby bench. "Shall we sit?"

They settled onto the bench, surrounded by the quiet hum of the town. For a moment, they simply watched their breath rise in small clouds into the chilly air.

"I've been thinking a lot about our conversations," Klaus began, his gaze fixed on the tree lights. "About your dreams, your worries… and mine too."

Merry turned to him, her voice steady. "I've been thinking too—about the bakery, my future… and you."

Klaus looked at her with a softness that made her feel truly seen. "In all my years," he said, "I've never met anyone like you, Merry. Your dedication to your family's legacy, your warmth—it's inspiring."

Merry blushed slightly. "And I've never met anyone like you either, Klaus. You're…" She laughed softly, searching for words. "You're literally magical."

They shared a smile, the moment lightened by the admission.

"But you also understand me," she continued, "in a way I didn't know was possible."

As they shared their fears and dreams, Merry felt the weight on her shoulders lift. Klaus's words held a reassurance that resonated deeply within her.

"You have a gift, Merry," he said, his tone sincere. "The way you bring joy to others and embrace this community… it's special."

Merry felt a surge of courage. "Thank you, Klaus. I think I needed to hear that."

Merry glanced at the town square around them, her gaze landing back on Klaus. "You know, I think I've finally realized something. The bakery isn't just my grandmother's legacy—it's become my own. And Tannenbaum Falls…" She smiled, a sense of peace settling over her. "It feels like home."

Klaus nodded. "This town does have a way of weaving magic into people's lives."

Merry laughed softly. "I think you might have worked a little of your own magic on me too."

Klaus raised an eyebrow, a hint of amusement in his expression. "Oh? And what kind of magic would that be?"

"The kind that makes me want to stay," she replied, her voice quiet but certain. "With the bakery, with Tannenbaum Falls... and with you."

Klaus seemed momentarily taken aback, but then he gently cupped her face, his touch warm against her skin. "I feel the same way," he murmured.

They shared a tender embrace, a sense of calm washing over Merry. In that moment, surrounded by the lights of Tannenbaum Falls, she knew she had found where she truly belonged.

Snowflakes drifted down as Merry and Klaus strolled along Main Street, fingers intertwined. The familiar sights around her seemed new, filled with a sense of wonder and joy.

"You know," she mused, glancing up at the lights, "it's like I'm seeing this town for the first time all over again."

Klaus smiled. "That's the magic of Christmas. It has a way of making everything feel new."

As they passed by Millie's bakery, the scent of cinnamon and vanilla wafted through the air, wrapping around them like a warm hug. Merry paused, a thought sparking in her mind.

"You know," she said, turning to Klaus with a playful grin, "I think I've got an idea for a new cookie recipe. Care to be my official taste tester?"

Klaus chuckled. "I'd be honored. Though I should warn you—I've developed quite the discerning taste from centuries of sampling Mrs. Claus's baking."

Merry laughed, nudging him lightly. "Challenge accepted, Mr. Krampus."

They continued their walk, the peacefulness of the night settling around them. As they passed familiar shops adorned with festive decorations, Merry felt a quiet gratitude fill her. She thought about the journey that had led her here, the doubts she'd faced, and the unexpected joy she'd found in this town—and in Klaus.

"Klaus," she began softly, her tone more serious, "do you ever wonder about the future? About how we'll make this work with... well, with your unique situation?"

Klaus paused, turning to face her fully. His expression was calm, a quiet conviction in his gaze. "Merry, in all my years, I've learned that love is the strongest magic there is. It can overcome any challenge, bridge any gap. As long as we're together, I have no doubts."

Merry's heart swelled at his words, and a sense of peace washed over her. "You're right," she whispered. "Together, we can do anything."

Hand in hand, they continued their walk, letting the magic of the evening wrap around them. The lights of Tannenbaum Falls seemed to shine even brighter, a reflection of the love and hope filling their hearts. And with each step they took, Merry felt more certain that she'd not only found love but a true partner in life's grand adventure.

As the gentle glow of the lights illuminated the town square, Merry and Klaus strolled arm-in-arm through the frosty air. Snow dusted the quiet streets, settling softly around them. Just as they neared Town Hall, a voice from an open window caught their attention.

"We can't let the festival get too folksy, Councilman," Mayor Harlow's baritone declared. "New regulations will ensure we maintain the town's image as a pristine holiday destination."

Merry exchanged a glance with Klaus, her heartbeat quickening. "They're planning changes to the festival," she whispered, a mix of disbelief and frustration brewing inside her.

Klaus gave a solemn nod. "Seems our traditions might be in jeopardy."

With a determined breath, Merry marched up the steps of Town Hall, Klaus following with quiet resolve. Inside, the warmth stood in stark contrast to the winter chill as they made their way toward Mayor Harlow's office. "Mayor Harlow!" she called, her voice firm.

The mayor, caught off guard, emerged with an eyebrow raised. "Miss North?" he greeted, looking between her and Klaus. "To what do I owe this unexpected visit?"

Merry's voice steadied as she spoke. "I overheard talk about festival changes. I'm concerned about how new regulations could disrupt the traditions that make our festival—and this town—so unique."

The mayor's expression shifted, the usual warmth replaced by a more businesslike demeanor. "Merry," he began, his tone patronizing, "change is necessary for progress. We're adapting to bring Tannenbaum Falls into the future."

Merry's brow furrowed. "Mayor, our traditions are the heart of this community. They're why people visit, and more importantly, they're what makes us who we are. There must be a way to balance growth and tradition."

Mayor Harlow shook his head. "Quaint, yes, but dated. To draw larger crowds, we need modern attractions—light shows, a celebrity guest, perhaps even a small winter wonderland park."

Before Merry could respond, Klaus took a step forward, his voice steady and resonant. "Mayor, with all due respect, the true magic of Christmas doesn't come from spectacles. It's found in community, in the small moments and traditions that connect us."

Merry glanced at Klaus, grateful for his support, and continued, "Tannenbaum Falls isn't about big-budget attractions. It's about people, history, and the little things that make this place feel like home."

The mayor paused, perhaps caught off guard by the conviction in their voices. "Well," he said slowly, "I suppose we could review the regulations."

"That's all I ask," Merry replied, a note of hope in her voice. "Give us the chance to show you how important these traditions are to everyone."

As she spoke, she felt Klaus's steady presence beside her, filling her with renewed confidence.

The next morning, Merry and Klaus found themselves strategizing at the community center with a small group of volunteers. The room was buzzing with excitement and a touch of nervous energy as they discussed their vision for an event that would demonstrate their balanced approach to the festival.

"We'll need activities that capture both the spirit of tradition and something new," Merry said, jotting down notes as the others nodded in agreement.

"How about a workshop where people can make their own ornaments?" Mrs. Tinsel suggested. "It's hands-on and keeps things authentic."

Klaus nodded approvingly. "And perhaps a new element to draw families—like guided history tours of Tannenbaum Falls. It could emphasize the town's unique stories."

Merry looked around at the eager faces of her neighbors, her heart swelling with gratitude. "Everyone, thank you. This wouldn't be possible without your dedication. Let's make this festival unforgettable."

With that, they broke off into smaller groups, each person diving into their tasks with renewed enthusiasm.

Over the next week, Merry and Klaus worked tirelessly alongside the volunteers, the town square transforming day by day. Handmade decorations lined the booths, local crafters contributed to displays, and preparations for the cookie exchange and caroling contest were well underway.

One evening, as Merry and Klaus surveyed the nearly-finished setup, Mayor Harlow approached, his gaze assessing. He walked the length of the square, his steps slow and thoughtful.

"Miss North, Klaus," he greeted, nodding at the festive scene. "It appears you've managed to create quite a display. People are talking about it."

Merry took a breath, choosing her words carefully. "Mayor, this is what Tannenbaum Falls is about—our history, our people, and traditions. It's not flashy, but it's meaningful."

Klaus added, "You asked for something memorable, and this is it. It's a true reflection of Tannenbaum Falls."

The mayor's gaze lingered on a handmade wreath, his expression softening just a little. "It does seem...authentic," he admitted slowly. "And the townspeople do appear to be engaged."

Merry couldn't contain her smile. "Thank you, Mayor. We want to honor our history while still welcoming visitors."

Mayor Harlow cleared his throat, looking both touched and reluctant. "Well, carry on, then. We'll see how this pans out," he replied gruffly, but a slight nod of approval followed as he left.

The festival day dawned bright and cold, the square filled with the sounds of carols, the scent of warm cider, and the laughter of children playing in the fresh snow. Merry, bundled up in her coat and scarf, watched as families gathered at the booths, volunteers handed out cookies, and the townspeople shared in the joy they'd all worked to create.

Klaus approached her, carrying two steaming mugs of cocoa. "Looks like we've done it," he said, passing her one with a soft smile.

Merry took a sip, savoring the warmth and sweetness. "Together," she agreed, her voice filled with satisfaction.

As the sun began to set, casting a golden glow over the square, Merry found herself by the Christmas tree, Klaus by her side. People milled around, admiring the decorations and singing along to the carolers. It was exactly the festive scene she'd dreamed of preserving.

Klaus looked at her, his voice low. "Merry, this town—this festival—it wouldn't be what it is without you. You've given everyone here a reason to believe in what we have."

Merry felt a warmth blossom in her chest, beyond the chill in the air. "And you've reminded me why this matters," she replied softly, glancing up at the tree, then back at him.

As the carolers started up again, the townsfolk joined in, their voices filling the air in a harmonious blend. Merry looked around, feeling an immense pride swell within her. They had done it; they had brought the heart of Tannenbaum Falls to life.

She glanced back at Klaus, grateful and more certain than ever that she was right where she was meant to be—standing beside him, surrounded by the community she loved, under the glow of twinkling lights that held the promise of many more Christmases to come.

# Chapter 11

Merry's boots crunched through the freshly fallen snow as she hurried across the festival grounds, her breath coming in quick puffs of white vapor. The twinkling lights and cheerful decorations blurred past her as she scanned the crowd, searching for one face in particular.

"Excuse me," she murmured, weaving between families admiring gingerbread houses and children eagerly lining up to visit Santa. The scent of cinnamon and pine needles filled the air, but Merry barely noticed, her heart pounding with anticipation.

Where could he be? she wondered, tugging her scarf tighter against the chill. Klaus had to be here somewhere – the festival was his pride and joy, after all. As she rounded a corner past a hot cocoa stand, Merry caught a glimpse of dark hair and broad shoulders that made her pulse quicken.

There he was, standing near the grand Christmas tree at the center of the square. Klaus's tall frame was hunched slightly as he conferred with a group of elves – or rather, local teenagers dressed as elves. His brow was furrowed in concentration, and Merry could see the tension in his jaw even from a distance.

"No, no, the star needs to be straightened," Klaus was saying, gesturing emphatically at the treetop. "And where are the candy canes for the lower branches? We can't have bare spots."

One of the elves scurried off, nearly dropping his jingling hat in his haste. Klaus ran a hand through his hair, leaving it charmingly tousled.

Merry's heart gave a little flip at the sight. Even stressed and serious, he was breathtakingly handsome.

"Klaus," she called out softly, taking a step closer. But her voice was lost in the bustling crowd and cheerful holiday music. Merry hesitated, suddenly unsure. Should she interrupt him when he was clearly so focused on last-minute preparations?

Before she could decide, Klaus turned slightly, his gaze sweeping the festival grounds. For a moment, Merry thought his eyes met hers, and she felt a spark of connection. But then he was turning away again, barking out another order to his harried helpers.

Merry's shoulders slumped. She'd been so eager to talk to him, to clear the air between them. But now she wondered if she'd made a mistake in coming here. Klaus clearly had his hands full with the festival. Maybe this wasn't the right time after all.

Merry took a deep breath, steeling her nerves. No, she had to do this now. Their relationship was too important to let doubts fester. With renewed determination, she wove through the crowd, her heart hammering in her chest.

"Klaus," she called out, louder this time. Her voice wavered slightly, a mix of excitement and apprehension coloring her tone.

Klaus turned, his eyes widening in surprise. "Merry? What are you doing here?"

She reached him, breathless. "I needed to talk to you. I know you're busy, but—"

"Of course," Klaus said, his brow furrowing. "Is everything alright?"

Merry hesitated, glancing at the curious elves nearby. "Can we go somewhere a little more private?"

Klaus nodded, leading her to a quiet corner behind a giant gingerbread house. The scent of cinnamon and sugar enveloped them, a stark contrast to the tension Merry felt building inside her.

"Klaus, I—" she started, then faltered. How could she express her fears without sounding selfish? "I'm worried about us. About you. It feels like the festival has become your whole world lately."

Klaus's eyes softened. "Merry, I'm sorry if I've been distant. This event means so much to the town, to the children. I just want everything to be perfect."

"I understand that," Merry said, twisting her hands together. "But what about us? Our plans? We've barely seen each other in weeks."

Klaus reached out, gently taking her hands in his. "You're right. I've been consumed by the preparations. But please believe me when I say you're still the most important part of my life."

Merry felt a glimmer of hope, but uncertainty still gnawed at her. "Then why does it feel like you're slipping away?"

Merry's eyes welled with tears as Klaus's words echoed in her mind. "The most important part of my life," he'd said, but his actions spoke louder. She pulled her hands away, her voice trembling.

"If I'm so important, why am I always an afterthought? You say one thing, but your actions..." She shook her head, auburn hair falling across her face. "Maybe the festival is what truly matters to you."

Klaus's brow furrowed deeper, his old-world charm faltering as he struggled to find the right words. "Merry, please. You must understand. The festival is my duty, but you—"

"Your duty," Merry interrupted, her warm green eyes now stormy with hurt. "That's all I am to you, isn't it? Another responsibility?"

"No, that's not what I meant," Klaus protested, reaching for her again. But Merry stepped back, her heart breaking with each word.

"I can't do this anymore, Klaus. I won't compete with centuries of tradition." With that, she turned and fled, tears streaming down her cheeks as she pushed through the crowd of festive onlookers.

Klaus stood rooted to the spot, his hand still outstretched. The jovial sounds of the festival faded to a dull roar in his ears as he watched Merry's retreating form. Confusion and frustration warred within him, his centuries of wisdom offering no solace in this moment.

"What just happened?" he muttered to himself, running a hand through his dark hair. The scent of gingerbread, once comforting, now seemed to mock him. How had his attempt to reassure Merry gone so terribly wrong?

Merry stumbled through the festive throng, her vision blurred by tears. She found herself in a secluded corner of the festival grounds, nestled between two towering evergreens. The cheerful sounds of laughter and carols felt distant now, muffled by her swirling emotions.

She sank onto a wooden bench, its rough surface cool against her palms. "What have I done?" she whispered, her breath forming small clouds in the crisp air. The scent of pine surrounded her, a bittersweet reminder of the Christmas spirit she usually cherished.

Across the grounds, Klaus stood frozen, his eyes fixed on the spot where Merry had disappeared. The weight of centuries pressed down on him, heavier than ever before. He glanced at the half-finished toy train in his hands, then back to the bustling crowd.

"Herr Krampus!" a cheerful voice called. "We need your expertise with the carousel!"

Klaus's jaw clenched. He set the toy down with trembling hands. "I... I'm afraid I must attend to something else," he said, his voice strained.

The festival organizer's face fell. "But sir, the children—"

"The children will understand," Klaus interrupted, softer this time. He met the organizer's eyes. "Some things are more important than tradition."

With that, Klaus strode purposefully into the crowd, his heart racing. "Where are you, Merry?" he murmured, searching for a glimpse of auburn hair among the sea of festive hats and scarves. "I cannot lose you now."

Merry closed her eyes, letting the memories wash over her like a warm breeze. She saw Klaus's gentle smile as he taught her to carve a tiny wooden reindeer, his strong hands guiding hers. The image shifted to their first snowball fight, his deep laughter echoing through the trees as she landed a perfect hit on his shoulder. Her heart ached with longing.

"Oh, Klaus," she whispered, a tear sliding down her cheek. "Did I throw away something magical?"

"Penny for your thoughts, dear?" a familiar voice called out.

Merry looked up to see Clara Miller approaching, her kind eyes twinkling with concern. The older woman settled beside her on the bench, the scent of cinnamon and cloves clinging to her cozy sweater.

"It's nothing, Clara," Merry said, hastily wiping her eyes. "Just... holiday stress, I suppose."

Clara chuckled softly. "In all my years in Tannenbaum Falls, I've never known 'nothing' to bring such sadness to those lovely green eyes of yours." She patted Merry's hand. "Now, why don't you tell old Clara what's really troubling you?"

Merry hesitated, then sighed. "It's Klaus. I think I've made a terrible mistake."

"Ah," Clara nodded sagely. "The Toymaker. He's a complicated soul, that one."

"I thought I knew what I wanted," Merry continued, her voice quavering. "But now I'm not so sure. What if I've ruined everything?"

Clara's expression softened. "My dear, in matters of the heart, there's rarely such a thing as 'ruined.' Bruised, perhaps. But never beyond repair."

Merry looked up, hope flickering in her eyes. "You really think so?"

"I know so," Clara replied with a wink. "Now, tell me about these happy memories you were lost in just now."

Klaus trudged through the snow-dusted festival grounds, his brow furrowed in contemplation. The twinkling lights and cheerful decorations seemed to mock his troubled heart. He found himself drawn to Arthur's workshop, a quaint wooden structure nestled at the edge of the square.

"Arthur?" Klaus called out, rapping his knuckles against the weathered door.

The old craftsman's voice drifted from within. "Come in, come in!"

Klaus stepped inside, enveloped by the comforting scent of pine and wood shavings. Arthur stood at his workbench, carefully sanding a delicate wooden ornament.

"Ah, Klaus," Arthur said, setting down his tools. "What brings you here with such a heavy heart?"

Klaus sighed, running a hand through his dark hair. "Is it that obvious?"

Arthur chuckled softly. "To these old eyes? Clear as day."

"It's Merry," Klaus confessed, leaning against the workbench. "I fear I've made a terrible mistake."

Arthur nodded sagely. "Matters of the heart are rarely simple, my boy. Tell me, what troubles you?"

As Klaus poured out his story, Arthur listened intently, his weathered hands continuing to work on the ornament. When Klaus finished, the old craftsman set down his creation and fixed him with a thoughtful gaze.

"You know," Arthur began, stroking his gray beard, "I was once faced with a similar choice. My craft or my love."

Klaus's eyes widened. "What did you do?"

Arthur smiled, a hint of sadness in his eyes. "I chose my work, believing it was my duty. It wasn't until years later that I realized my mistake."

"And then?" Klaus asked, hanging on every word.

"By then, it was too late," Arthur said softly. "Don't make the same mistake I did, Klaus. Follow your heart before it's too late."

Klaus stood in silence, Arthur's words echoing in his mind. The weight of his choices pressed down on him, and he realized with startling clarity how much Merry meant to him.

"Thank you, Arthur," Klaus said, his voice thick with emotion. "I think I know what I need to do."

As Klaus hurried out of the workshop, his heart pounding with newfound determination, he couldn't shake the image of Merry's tear-stained face. The thought of losing her forever filled him with a deep, aching dread.

Across the festival grounds, Merry sat alone on a bench, her fingers absently tracing the pattern on her grandmother's cookie tin. She thought of Klaus's warm smile, the way his eyes lit up when he talked about his toys, and the gentle strength of his embrace.

"Oh, Klaus," she whispered to herself, her breath visible in the cold air. "How did we let things get so complicated?"

As the festival bustled around them, both Merry and Klaus found themselves at a crossroads, each realizing that the magic of Christmas wasn't just in the twinkling lights or festive decorations, but in the love they shared. The question now was whether they could find their way back to each other before it was too late.

The festival lights twinkled in the gathering dusk, casting a warm glow over the snow-dusted grounds. Klaus strode purposefully through the crowd, his eyes scanning for a glimpse of auburn hair. His heart raced, each step bringing him closer to Merry—and to the moment that could change everything.

Suddenly, he spotted her. Merry stood near the giant Christmas tree, her green eyes shimmering with unshed tears as she gazed up at the star-topped pinnacle. Klaus's breath caught in his throat.

"Merry!" he called out, his voice carrying over the festive music.

She turned, her eyes widening as she saw him approaching. "Klaus? What are you—"

Before she could finish, a loud crack echoed through the air. The crowd gasped as the massive tree began to tilt precariously, ornaments tinkling ominously.

"Look out!" Klaus shouted, lunging forward.

In a heartbeat, he reached Merry, wrapping his arms around her protectively as the tree crashed down behind them. They stumbled, Klaus's momentum carrying them both to the ground.

For a moment, they lay there, breathless and stunned. Klaus looked down at Merry, their faces inches apart. "Are you alright?" he asked softly, concern etched across his features.

Merry nodded, her eyes locked on his. "You... you saved me," she whispered.

As they gazed at each other, the world around them faded away. The misunderstandings, the hurt, the doubts—all seemed to dissolve in that instant.

But before either could speak, a commotion erupted around them. Festival-goers rushed to help, voices raised in alarm. Klaus reluctantly helped Merry to her feet, their moment broken.

"We need to talk," he said urgently, taking her hand.

Merry nodded, hope blooming in her chest. "Yes, we do."

Just then, the festival organizer appeared, his face panic-stricken. "Klaus! We need you immediately. The tree, the lights—everything's in chaos!"

Klaus hesitated, torn between his duty and his heart. He looked at Merry, anguish clear in his eyes.

"Go," Merry said softly, squeezing his hand. "We'll talk later."

As Klaus was pulled away by the frantic organizer, he called back, "Meet me at the old clocktower at midnight. Please, Merry. It's important."

Merry watched him disappear into the crowd, her heart racing. Would midnight bring a new beginning—or a final goodbye?

# Chapter 12

The scent of cinnamon and vanilla wrapped around Merry like a warm hug as she sat alone at a corner table in Millie's bakery. She cradled a steaming mug of hot cocoa, watching snowflakes dance outside the frosted windows. The cheerful tinkling of bells on the door and the soft murmur of conversations filled the cozy space.

Merry's gaze drifted to the display case filled with her grandmother's famous Christmas cookies. A bittersweet smile tugged at her lips as she remembered Millie's words: "Baking isn't just about the ingredients, dear. It's about the love you put into every batch."

She took a sip of cocoa, savoring the rich chocolate flavor. "Oh, Grandma," Merry whispered, "I hope I'm doing your legacy justice."

Her eyes roamed over the festive decorations adorning the bakery—twinkling lights, garlands of evergreen, and cheery red bows. The sight filled her heart with a familiar warmth, reminding her of childhood Christmases spent helping Millie frost sugar cookies.

"Excuse me," a young boy's voice piped up, interrupting her reverie. "Are those reindeer cookies?"

Merry turned to see a freckle-faced child pointing eagerly at the display case. "They sure are! Would you like one?"

As she wrapped up a cookie for the boy, Merry felt a surge of gratitude. This bakery wasn't just a business—it was the heart of the community, bringing people together one sweet treat at a time.

Meanwhile, Klaus trudged through the snow-covered streets of Tannenbaum Falls, his footsteps leaving a solitary trail behind him. The town sparkled with holiday cheer, strings of lights twinkling from every eave and lamppost.

He paused, watching a group of children engaged in an enthusiastic snowball fight. Their laughter echoed through the crisp air, bringing a wistful smile to his face.

"Mr. Klaus!" one of the children called out, waving. "Come play with us!"

Klaus chuckled, shaking his head. "Perhaps another time, young ones. Enjoy your game."

As he continued his stroll, Klaus's thoughts turned inward. Centuries of spreading Christmas cheer weighed heavily on his shoulders. He longed for the simple joy those children possessed—the ability to find wonder in every snowflake, every twinkling light.

Passing by shop windows filled with festive displays, Klaus reflected on the true meaning of the season. It wasn't about the gifts or the decorations, but the connections forged between people. The love shared among family and friends. The sense of belonging to something greater than oneself.

He sighed, his breath visible in the frosty air. "If only they could see," he murmured, "the magic that lies in a simple act of kindness."

As Klaus approached the town square, his gaze was drawn to the warm glow emanating from Millie's bakery. Through the window, he caught a glimpse of Merry, her auburn hair catching the light as she smiled at a customer. For a moment, the weight on his shoulders seemed to lift, and he felt a spark of something he hadn't experienced in centuries—hope.

The crackling fire cast a warm glow across Merry's living room as she settled into her favorite armchair, a worn leather photo album resting on her lap. She ran her fingers over the embossed cover, tracing the words "Christmas Memories" before gently opening it.

"Oh, Grandma," Merry whispered, her green eyes misting as she gazed at a photo of her grandmother standing proudly in front of Millie's bakery. "I wish you could see it now."

She turned the page, chuckling at a picture of herself as a young girl, covered head to toe in flour. "I remember that day," she said softly. "You taught me how to make your famous snickerdoodles."

As she flipped through the pages, memories flooded back. The scent of cinnamon and vanilla seemed to fill the air, transporting her back to those cherished moments.

"I can almost hear your laugh," Merry murmured, touching a photo of her grandmother mid-giggle, a whisk in one hand and a mixing bowl in the other. "You always said baking was about love, not just ingredients."

She paused on a picture of the entire town gathered in the square, her grandmother at the center, distributing cookies. "You brought everyone together, didn't you? That's what I want to do too."

Merry closed the album, hugging it to her chest. "I hope I'm making you proud, Grandma. I'm trying to keep your spirit alive in every cookie I bake."

---

In his cozy workshop, Klaus stood surrounded by an array of wooden toys in various stages of completion. The scent of pine and varnish hung in the air as he ran his hand over the smooth curve of a rocking horse's back.

"Another year, another batch of toys," he mused, his voice tinged with both pride and melancholy. "But to what end?"

He picked up a small wooden train, turning it over in his hands. "For centuries, I've crafted these gifts, hoping to bring joy to children's hearts. But in this modern world, do they still hold the same magic?"

Klaus set the train down and moved to the window, gazing out at the snow-covered landscape. "I've witnessed countless Christmases, seen generations come and go. Yet here I stand, unchanged, unchanging."

He turned back to his workbench, eyes falling on an unfinished doll. "Perhaps it's time for a change," he murmured, picking up a small paintbrush. "To find a new purpose, a new connection."

As he began to paint delicate features on the doll's face, Klaus felt a familiar spark of creativity. "Maybe," he said softly, "just maybe, there's still a place for an old toymaker like me in this world. A chance to bring not just toys, but understanding and compassion."

Merry pressed her forehead against the cool glass of the window, her breath fogging the pane as she watched snowflakes dance in the twilight. The twinkling lights of Tannenbaum Falls sparkled in the distance, a picturesque scene that usually filled her with warmth. But tonight, a hint of uncertainty gnawed at her heart.

"Is this really where I'm meant to be?" she whispered to herself, her green eyes reflecting the falling snow.

She turned away from the window, her gaze falling on the mixing bowls and recipe cards scattered across the kitchen counter. The aroma of cinnamon and nutmeg still lingered in the air from her earlier baking session.

"Grandma's legacy," Merry mused, running her fingers along the worn edge of a recipe card. "But is it my legacy too?"

She picked up a cookie cutter shaped like a Christmas tree, turning it over in her hands. "I love this bakery, I do. But sometimes I wonder..."

Her voice trailed off as she set the cookie cutter down and reached for her phone. She pulled up a job listing she'd bookmarked earlier - a position at a prestigious bakery in the city.

"Maybe it's time to spread my wings," Merry said softly. "To see what else is out there."

She glanced back at the window, at the town she'd grown to love. "But then again, there's something special about this place. About the people here."

Merry sighed, conflict evident in her furrowed brow. "Oh, Grandma," she whispered. "I wish you were here to guide me. What would you say if you could see me now?"

Merry zipped up her coat and stepped out into the crisp winter air, her boots crunching on the freshly fallen snow. The twinkling lights of Tannenbaum Falls greeted her, strung between lampposts and adorning shop windows.

As she strolled down Main Street, the familiar sights and sounds of the town embraced her. Mr. Peterson was hanging a wreath on his hardware store door, and he waved cheerfully.

"Evening, Merry! Those gingerbread cookies you sent over were a hit with the grandkids!"

Merry's face lit up with a warm smile. "I'm so glad they enjoyed them, Mr. Peterson. It's Grandma's secret recipe."

She continued her walk, pausing to admire the intricate ice sculpture in front of the town hall. The sense of community enveloped her like a cozy blanket.

"It's not just about the bakery," Merry thought, her heart swelling. "It's about the connections, the shared joy. This town... it's part of me."

Meanwhile, across town, Klaus found himself drawn to the laughter echoing from Evergreen Park. He stood at the edge, watching children build snowmen and engage in friendly snowball fights.

A young girl struggled to roll a large snowball for her snowman's base. Without hesitation, Klaus approached.

"May I offer some assistance?" he asked gently.

The girl's face brightened. "Yes, please! I want to make the biggest snowman ever!"

As they worked together, Klaus felt a familiar warmth spreading through his chest. "You know," he said, his voice soft with wisdom, "the best snowmen are built with not just snow, but with kindness and teamwork."

The girl nodded seriously. "Like how you're helping me?"

Klaus smiled, his eyes crinkling at the corners. "Exactly like that. And perhaps, when you're older, you'll remember this moment and help someone else."

As they finished the snowman, Klaus stepped back, watching the children play with a mixture of joy and longing. "This," he thought, "this is what truly matters. Planting seeds of kindness that will grow for generations to come."

Merry sat at her cozy kitchen table, a steaming mug of cocoa beside her as she opened her leather-bound journal. Her pen hovered over the blank page for a moment before she began to write.

"Dear Diary," she murmured softly, her brow furrowing. "I love this town, I really do. But sometimes I wonder if I'm living up to Grandma's legacy. Am I doing enough? Can I make the bakery thrive and still find my own happiness?"

She paused, twirling a strand of auburn hair around her finger. "It's not just about cookies and hot chocolate. It's about creating a place where people feel at home. But where's my home? In the bakery, or somewhere else entirely?"

Across town, Klaus sat in his workshop, surrounded by half-finished wooden toys. He pulled out an ancient, worn journal and began to write, his elegant script flowing across the page.

"The children's laughter in the park today," he wrote, "it reminded me of simpler times. How do I bridge the gap between my duty and my desire for connection? Can I find a place in this modern world without losing sight of my purpose?"

As the sun began to set, painting the sky in hues of pink and orange, Merry decided to take a walk to clear her head. She bundled up in her favorite red coat and headed towards the town square.

Meanwhile, Klaus felt the pull to explore the town, his feet carrying him towards the heart of Tannenbaum Falls.

As Merry rounded the corner into the square, her eyes met Klaus's across the crowded space. For a moment, time seemed to stand still. She saw the same uncertainty, the same longing for belonging reflected in his eyes that she felt in her heart.

Their gazes held for a beat longer than usual, a silent understanding passing between them. Merry offered a small, tentative smile, which Klaus returned with a slight nod.

As they passed each other, Merry couldn't help but wonder, "Does he feel it too? This struggle to find our place?"

Klaus, his heart quickening, thought to himself, "Perhaps I'm not alone in this journey after all."

The moment passed, but the connection lingered, leaving both Merry and Klaus with a sense of possibility and a flicker of hope as they continued on their separate ways through the twinkling lights of the town square.

The warm glow of Café Noel beckoned Merry and Klaus from the chilly evening air. Merry pushed open the door, the cheerful jingle of bells announcing their arrival. The aroma of cinnamon and freshly brewed coffee enveloped them as they settled into a cozy corner booth.

"I'm glad we ran into each other," Merry said, her green eyes twinkling in the soft light. "I've been feeling a bit... lost lately."

Klaus nodded, his expression thoughtful. "As have I. It's curious how one can feel adrift even in a place as welcoming as Tannenbaum Falls."

Merry wrapped her hands around her steaming mug of hot chocolate. "Exactly. I love this town, but sometimes I wonder if I'm truly fulfilling my potential here."

"Ah, the eternal question of purpose," Klaus mused, his voice carrying a hint of centuries-old wisdom. "I've found myself pondering similar thoughts. How does one balance duty with personal fulfillment?"

As they talked, Merry felt a weight lifting from her shoulders. There was something comforting about Klaus's presence, a sense of understanding that went beyond words.

After finishing their drinks, they decided to take a stroll through Evergreen Park. Snow crunched beneath their feet as they walked side by side, their breaths visible in the crisp air.

## A Very Krampus Christmas

"You know," Merry said, breaking the comfortable silence, "I never expected to find someone who understands these feelings so well."

Klaus's lips curved into a gentle smile. "Nor did I. Perhaps we were meant to cross paths, to remind each other that we're not alone in our struggles."

As they continued their walk, Merry realized that in Klaus, she had found not just a friend, but a kindred spirit. And for Klaus, the warmth of connection he felt with Merry was a balm to his centuries-old soul.

The snow-dusted bench in Evergreen Park beckoned to Merry and Klaus, offering a quiet spot to rest. As they sat down, their hands found each other, fingers intertwining naturally. The touch sent a warmth through Merry that had nothing to do with her mittens.

"Klaus," Merry began, her green eyes meeting his deep, wise gaze. "I've been thinking about what we discussed. About our fears and insecurities."

Klaus nodded, giving her hand a gentle squeeze. "As have I, my dear Merry."

She took a deep breath, the crisp winter air filling her lungs. "I want you to know that I'm here for you. Whatever challenges we face, we can face them together."

A smile tugged at Klaus's lips, his eyes crinkling at the corners. "Your words warm my heart more than you know. I, too, am committed to standing by your side."

Merry felt a surge of emotion, her voice wavering slightly as she continued. "Running Grandma's bakery, preserving traditions, finding my place in this town - it all seems less daunting when I know I have your support."

"And your presence gives me hope," Klaus responded, his voice carrying the weight of centuries. "In you, I've found a connection I've long sought. A reminder of the joy and love that this season truly represents."

As they sat there, hands clasped and hearts open, Merry marveled at how quickly Klaus had become an essential part of her life. The twinkling lights of Tannenbaum Falls seemed to shine a little brighter, reflecting the hope blooming in her heart.

Overwhelmed by emotion, Merry leaned into Klaus, wrapping her arms around him. He returned the embrace, enveloping her in warmth that defied the winter chill. Snowflakes drifted lazily around them, as if nature itself was celebrating their connection.

"Together," Merry whispered, her face nestled against Klaus's chest, "we can face anything."

Klaus's voice rumbled softly as he replied, "Indeed, my dear. With you by my side, I feel a renewed sense of purpose."

As they held each other, Merry felt a surge of determination. The challenges ahead no longer seemed insurmountable. With Klaus's support and her own resilience, she knew she could navigate the path before her, balancing tradition with her own dreams.

The embrace lingered, neither wanting to break the moment. In each other's arms, they found strength, understanding, and a promise of something beautiful blossoming between them.

Merry and Klaus rose from the bench, their fingers naturally intertwining as they began to stroll along the snow-dusted path. The soft crunch of snow beneath their feet created a gentle rhythm, matching the steady beating of their hearts.

"You know," Merry said, her green eyes twinkling with mirth, "I never thought I'd be holding hands with a Christmas spirit. It's not exactly something they prepare you for in baking school."

Klaus chuckled, the sound warm and rich. "And I never imagined I'd find such joy in the company of a mortal baker. Life has a way of surprising us, doesn't it?"

As they walked, Merry noticed how the streetlights cast a soft glow on Klaus's face, accentuating his timeless features. She felt a rush of affection, mixed with a hint of wonder at the extraordinary turn her life had taken.

"Speaking of surprises," Merry mused, "how do you think the townspeople would react if they knew who you really are?"

Klaus raised an eyebrow, a mischievous glint in his eye. "Perhaps we should start small. Maybe I'll reveal my toy-making skills at the next town fair."

Merry laughed, the sound carrying on the crisp winter air. "Oh, I can see it now. 'Klaus Krampus: Toymaker Extraordinaire'. You'd be the talk of Tannenbaum Falls!"

As they continued their walk, Merry's thoughts drifted to the challenges ahead - running the bakery, honoring her grandmother's legacy, and now, navigating a relationship with a centuries-old Christmas spirit.

Yet, with Klaus by her side, those challenges felt more like exciting adventures.

"You know," Merry said softly, giving Klaus's hand a gentle squeeze, "I think Grandma would have loved you. She always said that the true magic of Christmas was in the connections we make."

Klaus smiled, his eyes reflecting years of wisdom and newfound hope. "Your grandmother sounds like a remarkable woman. I look forward to hearing more about her, and perhaps sharing some of my own stories from Christmases past."

As they rounded the corner, the twinkling lights of Tannenbaum Falls stretched out before them, a shimmering tapestry of holiday cheer. Merry felt a surge of contentment, knowing that whatever lay ahead, she and Klaus would face it together.

# Chapter 13

Snowflakes drifted lazily past the frosted window of Millie's Bakery, each one a miniature work of art. Merry North gazed out at the wintry scene, barely registering the cozy warmth of the shop or the tempting aroma of cinnamon and vanilla that hung in the air. Her fingers absently traced the rim of her untouched mug of hot cocoa as her thoughts swirled like the falling snow.

Klaus. His name echoed in her mind, bringing with it a tangle of emotions she couldn't quite unravel. Merry's chest tightened as she recalled their last conversation, the words they'd left unspoken hanging between them like a heavy curtain.

"Why does everything have to be so complicated?" she muttered, tucking a wayward strand of auburn hair behind her ear.

The cheerful jingle of the bakery's bell cut through Merry's brooding. She turned, startled, as a whirlwind of youthful energy burst through the door.

"Miss Merry! Miss Merry!" Tommy Jenkins called out, his blond hair dusted with snow and his cheeks flushed from the cold. He skidded to a stop in front of her table, blue eyes sparkling with excitement.

Despite her melancholy mood, Merry couldn't help but smile at the boy's enthusiasm. "Well, hello there, Tommy. What's got you all worked up on this snowy afternoon?"

Tommy bounced on his toes, words tumbling out in a rush. "I've got the most amazing idea for a Christmas surprise for my friends, but I need your help! It's gonna be the best gift ever!"

## A Very Krampus Christmas

Merry's eyebrows rose in curiosity. "Oh really? And what sort of help does this amazing surprise require?"

"It's a secret," Tommy said, lowering his voice conspiratorially. "But I promise it'll be magical. Will you help me, Miss Merry? Pretty please?"

For a moment, Merry hesitated. Her heart was heavy with her own troubles, and she wasn't sure she had the energy for Tommy's schemes. But as she looked into his hopeful face, she felt a small spark of warmth kindle in her chest.

Maybe this is just what I need, she thought. A distraction from all this business with Klaus.

"Alright, Tommy," Merry said, her smile growing more genuine. "You've piqued my curiosity. Tell me more about this top-secret Christmas surprise of yours."

Tommy's face lit up with unbridled joy. He scrambled onto the chair across from Merry, leaning in close as if sharing state secrets.

"Okay, so here's the plan," he whispered excitedly. "I want to make a super special snow globe that shows all of Tannenbaum Falls at Christmas time! With the big tree in the square, and Millie's bakery, and even Mr. Klaus's toy workshop!"

Merry's eyes widened. "That sounds lovely, Tommy. But how do you plan to fit our whole town into a snow globe?"

"That's where the magic comes in!" Tommy exclaimed, his voice rising with enthusiasm. "We'll make it tiny, but perfect. Like a little Christmas wonderland you can hold in your hand!"

As Tommy described his vision, Merry found herself swept up in his excitement. She could almost see the miniature town, twinkling with festive lights, nestled safely within a glass sphere.

"It's not just a gift," Tommy continued, his eyes shining. "It's like... giving them a piece of home they can keep forever."

Merry's breath caught in her throat. Suddenly, she wasn't just seeing Tommy's snow globe - she was seeing her own situation with startling clarity. Wasn't that exactly what she wanted? To preserve the magic of Tannenbaum Falls, to share it with others... to create something lasting and beautiful with Klaus?

"You know, Tommy," Merry said softly, her mind whirling with new possibilities, "I think you might be onto something truly special here."

Merry's eyes swept across the bakery, spotting the items they'd need. "Alright, Tommy, let's gather our supplies. We'll need a glass jar, some glitter, and... oh! I have the perfect miniature figurines in the back room."

Tommy bounced on his toes, his blond hair flopping with each excited hop. "This is gonna be so cool! Can we use that sparkly blue glitter? It'll look just like the lake when it freezes over!"

Merry laughed, her warm green eyes crinkling at the corners. "Absolutely. And we'll need something to make the snow fall. I think I have just the thing."

As they collected their materials, Merry's thoughts drifted to Klaus. Would he appreciate a gesture like this? Something that captured the heart of their town?

"Miss Merry?" Tommy's voice pulled her back to the present. "Where should we set up?"

Merry glanced around, spotting a cozy nook near the window. "How about over there? We'll have plenty of light, and you can keep an eye out for your friends in case they walk by."

Tommy grinned mischievously. "Yeah, and I can duck if I see 'em coming! It's gotta be a surprise, you know."

They settled into their makeshift workstation, laying out their treasures. Merry watched as Tommy carefully arranged the tiny figurines inside the jar, his tongue poking out in concentration.

"Look!" he exclaimed. "There's the big Christmas tree, and Millie's bakery, and... oh! We can't forget Mr. Klaus's workshop!"

Merry's heart fluttered at the mention of Klaus. "You're right, Tommy. His workshop is an important part of our town."

As Tommy worked, Merry found herself lost in thought. Could she create something just as magical for Klaus? Something to show him how much he meant to her, and to Tannenbaum Falls?

Merry shook herself from her reverie and focused on the task at hand. "Alright, Tommy, now for the tricky part. We need to add the glitter and snowfall liquid very carefully."

Tommy's eyes widened with excitement. "Can I do it? Pretty please?"

Merry smiled warmly. "Of course, but let me guide you. We don't want a glitter explosion in Millie's bakery."

She gently took Tommy's hand, helping him sprinkle a pinch of glitter into the jar. "Easy does it," she murmured. "Just like dusting cookies with powdered sugar."

Tommy giggled. "But way more sparkly!"

Next, Merry uncapped the small bottle of snowfall liquid. "Now, we'll pour this in slowly. It's what makes the magic happen."

As they added the liquid, Merry couldn't help but think of the magic she'd felt with Klaus. The warmth of his smile, the gentleness in his eyes...

"Miss Merry?" Tommy's voice snapped her back to reality. "Is it done?"

Merry blinked, refocusing on the snow globe. "Let's see. Give it a gentle shake, Tommy."

Tommy carefully lifted the globe and gave it a soft shake. Instantly, a flurry of glitter and tiny white particles swirled around the miniature Tannenbaum Falls, creating a mesmerizing winter wonderland.

"Whoa," Tommy breathed, his face lighting up with pure joy. "It's like real snow!"

Merry felt a surge of warmth in her chest, Tommy's enthusiasm infectious. "It's beautiful, Tommy. You did an amazing job."

As they admired their handiwork, Merry realized something. This simple act of creating magic had brought her closer to Tommy, and in a way, closer to the spirit of Tannenbaum Falls itself.

"You know," she said softly, "sometimes the best gifts are the ones we make with our own hands and hearts."

Tommy nodded sagely. "Yeah, and this one's gonna knock their socks off!"

Merry wiped her flour-dusted hands on her apron, her mind suddenly made up. "Tommy, I think it's time I followed your example and made things right."

Tommy looked up from carefully wrapping the snow globe in tissue paper. "Huh? What d'you mean, Miss Merry?"

She knelt down to his level, her green eyes sparkling with newfound determination. "Remember Mr. Klaus? I need to talk to him, to fix something important. But I need your help. Can you keep our little creation a secret for now?"

"Sure thing!" Tommy's face lit up with excitement. "I'm great at keeping secrets! Well, except for that time I told everyone about Dad's surprise--"

Merry laughed, ruffling his tousled blond hair. "This one's different, okay? It's Christmas magic."

As they stepped out of Millie's bakery, the crisp winter air nipped at their cheeks. Merry tugged her scarf tighter, her heart pounding with anticipation.

"So, we're going to Mr. Klaus's workshop?" Tommy asked, his boots crunching satisfyingly in the fresh snow.

Merry nodded, her breath forming little clouds in the frosty air. "That's right. It's time to set things straight."

"Is he in trouble?" Tommy's blue eyes widened with concern.

"No, no," Merry assured him, chuckling softly. "Sometimes grown-ups just need to talk things out, like when you and your friends have a disagreement."

As they walked, Merry's thoughts raced. What would she say to Klaus? How would he react? The questions swirled in her mind like the glitter in their snow globe.

The workshop emerged from the snow-laden pines like a gingerbread house come to life. Merry paused at the foot of the wooden steps, her heart fluttering. Tommy tugged at her sleeve.

"Are you okay, Miss Merry? You look kinda pale."

She managed a smile. "Just a little nervous, that's all."

Merry ascended the steps, each creak under her boots matching her rising pulse. At the door, she hesitated, her hand hovering over the worn brass knocker.

"You can do it!" Tommy whispered encouragingly.

Drawing a deep breath, Merry rapped three times. The sound echoed in the stillness of the snowy forest.

Moments later, the door swung open. Klaus stood there, his dark hair slightly disheveled, a look of surprise etched on his striking features.

"Merry?" His deep voice carried a hint of concern. "Is everything alright?"

She gazed into his eyes, finding strength in their depths. "Klaus, I... we need to talk. Tommy here helped me realize something important."

Tommy waved enthusiastically. "Hi, Mr. Klaus! We made a super cool--"

"Tommy," Merry gently interrupted, "remember our secret?"

"Oh, right!" He mimed zipping his lips.

Klaus's brow furrowed with curiosity. "What's this about, Merry?"

She took another steadying breath. "It's about us, Klaus. About how sometimes the most precious things are right in front of us, waiting to be cherished. I don't want to let what we have slip away."

Klaus's stern expression softened as Merry spoke, her words melting the icy barrier between them. His eyes, usually guarded, now shimmered with a mix of surprise and tenderness. As she finished, Klaus reached out, taking her hand in his. His touch was warm and comforting, a stark contrast to the chilly air around them.

"Merry," he said, his voice low and earnest, "I... I want to work things out too. Please, come inside. Both of you."

As they stepped into the cozy workshop, the scent of pine and cinnamon enveloped them. Merry's gaze swept over the room, taking in the half-finished toys and intricate woodcarvings that spoke of Klaus's dedication to his craft.

Klaus guided them to a small sitting area near the crackling fireplace. "Tommy, would you mind tending to the fire for a moment?" he asked, a gentle smile playing on his lips.

As Tommy eagerly set about his task, Klaus turned to Merry. "I've been a fool," he admitted, his eyes never leaving hers. "I let my fears get the better of me."

Merry felt a lump form in her throat. "We both did, Klaus. I was so worried about preserving traditions that I almost lost sight of what truly matters."

Klaus nodded, squeezing her hand. "The traditions of Tannenbaum Falls are important, but not at the cost of our happiness. I realize now that together, we can honor the past while embracing the future."

Merry's heart swelled with hope. "That's exactly how I feel. But Klaus, what were you so afraid of?"

He sighed, his gaze momentarily drifting to the dancing flames. "I've seen so much change over the years. I was afraid that by opening my heart, I might lose myself, lose my purpose."

"Oh, Klaus," Merry whispered, her free hand reaching up to cup his cheek. "Your purpose is to bring joy and wonder to others. How could loving someone ever diminish that?"

As they talked, the tension between them melted away like snow in spring sunshine. They laughed about their misunderstandings, shared their deepest fears, and reaffirmed their commitment to each other and to the town they both cherished.

Tommy, who had been pretending not to listen, suddenly piped up, "Does this mean you two are gonna kiss now?"

Merry's cheeks flushed a deep crimson as she glanced at Tommy, then back to Klaus. His eyes twinkled with amusement, a warm smile spreading across his face.

"Well, young man," Klaus said, his voice carrying a hint of playfulness, "I believe that's a matter between Ms. North and myself."

Merry couldn't help but giggle, the sound light and carefree. She felt as though a great weight had been lifted from her shoulders. "Tommy, why don't you go check on that snow globe? Make sure it's set just right."

As Tommy scampered off, Merry turned back to Klaus. Her heart raced as she looked into his eyes, seeing centuries of wisdom and a depth of emotion that took her breath away.

"Klaus," she whispered, "I don't want to waste another moment. Will you come to the Tannenbaum Falls Winter Festival with me?"

He pulled her closer, his strong arms enveloping her in a warm embrace. "My dear Merry, I wouldn't miss it for the world."

Merry melted into his embrace, feeling safe and cherished. As she rested her head against his chest, she could hear the steady rhythm of his heartbeat. "We make quite a pair, don't we? The cookie baker and the toymaker."

Klaus chuckled, the sound rumbling through his chest. "Indeed we do. And together, we'll make this the most magical Christmas Tannenbaum Falls has ever seen."

As they stood there, wrapped in each other's arms, Merry knew that whatever challenges lay ahead, they would face them together, hand in hand, their love as enduring as the spirit of Christmas itself.

# Chapter 14

Merry's breath caught in her throat as she stepped onto the festival grounds. The air sparkled with twinkling lights and the scent of cinnamon and pine. Festive melodies drifted on the crisp winter breeze, mingling with the cheerful chatter of the townsfolk.

"Oh, Grandma," Merry whispered, "if only you could see this." She imagined her grandmother's twinkling eyes and warm smile, picturing how proud she'd be of Tannenbaum Falls' enduring holiday spirit.

As Merry wove through the crowd, the crunch of snow beneath her boots was drowned out by excited voices and laughter. Children darted past, their cheeks rosy with excitement, while vendors called out their wares – everything from steaming cups of cocoa to hand-carved wooden ornaments.

Pausing to admire an intricately decorated gingerbread house, Merry's gaze drifted across the festival. That's when she spotted him – Mayor Harlow, his portly figure unmistakable even at a distance. He stood near the town square's grand Christmas tree, deep in conversation with a group of councilmen.

Merry's heart began to race. This was her chance. She took a deep breath, steadying herself. "You can do this," she murmured, squaring her shoulders. "For the bakery. For the town."

With newfound determination, Merry began to make her way through the throng. She politely sidestepped a group of carolers and ducked under a string of garland being hung by volunteers.

"Excuse me," she said with a smile, gently maneuvering past a couple admiring a display of hand-blown glass ornaments. "Pardon me, just need to squeeze by."

As she drew closer to the mayor, Merry rehearsed her arguments in her head. She believed in the power of tradition, yes, but also in the importance of growth and inclusivity. Surely, there was a way to honor the past while embracing the future?

With each step, Merry's resolve strengthened. The strict regulations threatened not just her grandmother's legacy, but the very heart of what made Tannenbaum Falls special. She had to make Mayor Harlow understand that sometimes, the most precious traditions were the ones that evolved with love and care.

"Mayor Harlow!" Merry called out, her voice carrying over the festive din. The portly man turned, his bushy eyebrows rising in surprise as he caught sight of her. This was it. The moment of truth. Merry took a final deep breath and stepped forward, ready to fight for the soul of her beloved town.

Merry's breath caught in her throat as Mayor Harlow's stern gaze fell upon her. His imposing figure, draped in a festive red and green plaid suit, seemed to command the very air around him. She swallowed hard, her grandmother's warm smile flashing in her mind, giving her courage.

"Mayor Harlow," Merry said, her voice steadier than she felt. "I was hoping we could talk about the festival regulations."

The mayor's mustache twitched. "Ah, Miss North. I trust you're enjoying our little celebration?"

Merry glanced around at the twinkling lights and cheerful decorations. "It's beautiful, sir. But I'm worried we're losing something important in all these rules."

Mayor Harlow's brow furrowed. "Rules maintain order, Miss North. They preserve our traditions."

"But sir," Merry pressed, her green eyes sparkling with passion, "isn't the heart of our tradition the sense of community? The love we share?"

As she spoke, Merry could smell the sweet scent of cinnamon and pine needles wafting through the air. It reminded her of baking with her grandmother, of the joy they'd shared in creating something special for others.

"You see," she continued, gesturing to the bustling crowd around them, "every person here has a story, a connection to this town. My grandmother's bakery has been part of that for generations. These strict regulations... they're stifling the very spirit we're trying to preserve."

Mayor Harlow's expression softened slightly, but he still looked unconvinced. Merry knew she had to make him understand. She took a deep breath, ready to pour her heart into her words.

Merry's voice grew stronger, fueled by her conviction. "Mayor Harlow, I understand your desire to maintain the town's image, but at what cost? These regulations are pushing away the very people who make Tannenbaum Falls special."

The mayor's jaw tightened. "Miss North, I appreciate your enthusiasm, but these rules have kept our festival running smoothly for years. We can't simply throw them out because of... sentimentality."

Merry felt a flare of frustration, but she pushed it down. She had to make him see. "It's not just sentimentality, sir. It's the lifeblood of our community. Look around you."

She gestured to a nearby stall where an elderly woman was selling hand-knitted scarves. "Mrs. Thompson there has been coming to this festival for fifty years. Her scarves warm our necks and our hearts. But under the new rules, her stall barely made the cut."

Mayor Harlow's eyes followed her gesture, a flicker of uncertainty crossing his face. Merry pressed on, her voice rising with passion. "And over there, the Johnsons' hot chocolate stand. Their recipe has been passed down for generations. It's not just a drink, it's a tradition. But they're struggling to meet the new health code requirements."

As Merry spoke, she noticed heads turning in their direction. The festive chatter around them began to dim as people tuned into their conversation. She felt a surge of determination. This wasn't just about her anymore; it was about all of them.

"Mayor Harlow," Merry said, her voice carrying clearly now, "I'm not asking you to abandon all rules. I'm asking you to remember why we have this festival in the first place. It's about bringing people together, about love and community. Can't we find a way to preserve that spirit while still maintaining order?"

The crowd had grown silent now, all eyes on Merry and the mayor. Merry's heart pounded, but she stood tall, her gaze locked with Mayor Harlow's. She knew this moment could change everything, and she wasn't about to back down.

In the tense silence that followed, Merry's gaze drifted over the crowd. Suddenly, her breath caught in her throat. There, just a few yards away, stood Klaus, his dark eyes fixed on her with an intensity that made her heart skip a beat. His brow was furrowed with concern, but there was a glimmer of curiosity in his expression that gave her hope.

Merry hesitated, torn between continuing her impassioned plea to Mayor Harlow and the overwhelming desire to bridge the gap with Klaus. The toymaker's presence seemed to soften the edges of her determination, reminding her of the personal stakes involved.

"I... excuse me for just a moment, Mayor," Merry said, her voice suddenly gentle. She turned away from the bewildered official and made her way towards Klaus, her steps tentative but purposeful.

As she approached, Klaus's posture stiffened slightly, but he didn't retreat. Merry's heart raced as she stopped before him, close enough to catch the scent of pine and cinnamon that always seemed to cling to him.

"Klaus," she began, her voice barely above a whisper, "I know we've had our differences, but I can't do this alone. The town needs both of us, working together."

Klaus's eyebrows rose slightly, a mix of surprise and wariness in his eyes. "You seemed to be handling things quite well on your own, Miss North," he replied, his tone formal but not unkind.

Merry shook her head, a small smile tugging at her lips. "Maybe on the surface, but inside? I'm terrified. This isn't just about regulations, Klaus. It's about the heart of Tannenbaum Falls. And I think... I think you understand that better than anyone."

She watched as something shifted in Klaus's expression, the hard lines around his mouth softening. He glanced over her shoulder at Mayor Harlow, then back to her. "And what would you have us do?" he asked, his voice low and rich with centuries of wisdom.

Merry took a deep breath, hope blossoming in her chest. "Work with me," she said earnestly. "Help me show the Mayor that we can honor tradition while embracing change. Your voice, your experience... it could make all the difference."

For a moment, Klaus was silent, his eyes searching hers. Then, almost imperceptibly, he nodded. "Perhaps," he said slowly, "it is time for the old and the new to find common ground."

A wave of relief washed over Merry, and she resisted the urge to throw her arms around him. Instead, she smiled warmly, her eyes shining with gratitude. "Thank you, Klaus. Together, we can make this right."

As Merry and Klaus continued their conversation, the bustling festival around them seemed to fade away. The crowd, once abuzz with chatter and excitement, grew quieter, their attention drawn to the unlikely pair standing in their midst.

"I've been too rigid," Klaus admitted, his voice barely above a whisper. "Perhaps in my effort to preserve tradition, I've forgotten the true spirit of Christmas."

Merry's heart swelled with empathy. She reached out, gently touching Klaus's arm. "It's not about forgetting," she said softly. "It's about remembering why these traditions matter in the first place."

The scent of cinnamon and pine wafted through the air, a reminder of the festive atmosphere that surrounded them. Klaus's eyes, usually so guarded, now held a warmth that made Merry's breath catch.

"You remind me of someone," he murmured, a hint of a smile playing on his lips. "Someone who taught me the importance of love and community long ago."

Merry felt a blush creep up her cheeks. "I'm just trying to do what's right for Tannenbaum Falls," she said, her voice thick with emotion.

As they spoke, Mayor Harlow stood a few feet away, his brow furrowed in thought. The stern set of his shoulders began to relax as he watched Merry and Klaus, their words carrying on the crisp winter air.

"Perhaps," the Mayor muttered to himself, stroking his mustache, "I've been looking at this all wrong." He took a step back, his eyes widening as he truly saw the scene before him - not just a confrontation, but a community coming together.

The crowd surrounding them held their collective breath, the tension palpable in the frosty air. Merry felt the weight of their gazes, her heart pounding as she realized the gravity of this moment. She looked from Klaus to Mayor Harlow, seeing the conflict in their eyes.

"We all want what's best for Tannenbaum Falls," Merry said, her voice clear and strong. "But sometimes, what's best isn't found in rules and regulations. It's in the warmth of a neighbor's smile, the joy of shared traditions."

Klaus nodded, his eyes softening as he gazed at Merry. "She's right," he added, his deep voice carrying across the crowd. "I've seen countless Christmases, and the most memorable ones were never about perfection. They were about love and togetherness."

Mayor Harlow cleared his throat, adjusting his festive tie. "But without structure, how do we maintain our town's reputation?" he asked, his voice wavering slightly.

Merry smiled gently. "By embracing what makes us unique," she replied. "Our reputation should be built on the kindness of our people, not the strictness of our rules."

As she spoke, Merry noticed a shift in the atmosphere. The crowd began to murmur in agreement, nodding and exchanging knowing looks. She could feel the warmth of community spirit growing, melting away the icy barriers of regulation.

"What if," Merry suggested, her eyes twinkling with inspiration, "we focus on spreading joy rather than enforcing perfection? Imagine a festival where everyone contributes in their own special way."

The crowd's murmurs grew louder, excitement building. Klaus stepped forward, placing a supportive hand on Merry's shoulder. "I believe Merry's onto something," he said, a rare smile gracing his features. "This could be the start of a new tradition - one that honors our past while embracing our future."

Mayor Harlow's brow furrowed as he looked out at the sea of expectant faces. The weight of tradition battled with the undeniable energy of change in the air. He took a deep breath, his shoulders dropping as he made his decision.

"Well, I'll be," he chuckled, shaking his head. "Miss North, you've certainly stirred things up around here." He extended his hand to Merry. "I think it's time we loosen those regulations a bit. After all, what's Christmas without a little... magic?"

The crowd erupted in cheers as Merry shook the Mayor's hand, her green eyes sparkling with joy. "Thank you, Mayor Harlow," she said warmly. "I promise, we'll make this the best Tannenbaum Falls Christmas yet!"

## A Very Krampus Christmas

As the festival resumed with renewed vigor, Merry felt a gentle touch on her arm. She turned to find Klaus standing beside her, his usually stoic face softened by a tender smile.

"You did it," he murmured, his voice filled with admiration. "You've brought the true spirit of Christmas back to Tannenbaum Falls."

Merry blushed, tucking a strand of auburn hair behind her ear. "We did it," she corrected him. "I couldn't have done this without you, Klaus."

They stood side by side, watching as children gleefully decorated misshapen cookies and adults laughed over imperfectly wrapped gifts. The air was filled with the scent of cinnamon and pine, and the sound of carols sung slightly off-key.

Merry's heart swelled with happiness. This, she thought, is what Christmas is all about. She glanced at Klaus, catching his eye, and they shared a knowing smile. In that moment, she knew that their love for each other and for their town's traditions had truly triumphed.

Merry's heart fluttered as she gazed at Klaus, the twinkling lights of the festival reflecting in his eyes. The bustling sounds of laughter and merriment surrounded them, a stark contrast to the tension that had filled the air just moments ago.

"You know," Merry said, her voice soft and tinged with wonder, "I never imagined when I moved here that I'd be part of something so... magical."

Klaus chuckled, a warm, rich sound that sent a shiver down Merry's spine. "Tannenbaum Falls has a way of surprising people," he replied, his hand gently brushing against hers. "Especially those with hearts as open as yours."

Merry felt her cheeks warm at the compliment. She watched as a group of children raced by, their arms laden with freshly baked cookies from her grandmother's recipe. The sight filled her with a sense of pride and belonging.

"I think," she mused, more to herself than to Klaus, "this is what Grandma always meant when she talked about the spirit of Christmas. It's not about perfection, it's about coming together."

Klaus nodded, his expression thoughtful. "You've reminded us all of that, Merry. Even me."

As they stood there, shoulder to shoulder, Merry couldn't help but feel that this was just the beginning. The festival around them hummed with renewed energy, but more importantly, she sensed a shift in the town itself. A return to the warmth and inclusivity that had always been at its heart.

"So," she said, turning to Klaus with a mischievous glint in her eye, "what do you say we go decorate some imperfect cookies of our own?"

Klaus's laugh rang out, clear and joyful. "Lead the way, Miss North. I have a feeling this is going to be a Christmas to remember."

Hand in hand, they made their way through the crowd, ready to embrace whatever sweet surprises the season had in store for them.

# Chapter 15

Merry's heart fluttered like a trapped butterfly as she stood in the shadows backstage, the festive chatter of the Tannenbaum Falls Christmas Festival filtering through the heavy velvet curtain. She smoothed her hands over her emerald green dress, inhaling the mingled scents of pine, cinnamon, and peppermint that wafted through the air.

"Are you ready, my dear?" Klaus's deep, gentle voice broke through her reverie.

Merry turned to face him, drinking in the sight of his tall frame clad in a crisp white shirt and dark suit. His eyes, filled with centuries of wisdom, gazed at her with such tenderness that it made her breath catch.

"As ready as I'll ever be," she replied, managing a small smile. "Though I must admit, I'm more nervous than I was during my first gingerbread house competition."

Klaus chuckled softly, reaching out to take her hand. "You've nothing to fear, Merry. Your love for this town shines brighter than any star atop a Christmas tree."

The warmth of his touch sent a comforting tingle through her body, and Merry found herself leaning into him slightly. "You always know just what to say, don't you? It's almost like magic."

A mysterious smile played at the corners of Klaus's lips. "Perhaps it is, in its own way."

Before Merry could ponder his words further, the booming voice of the festival emcee rang out, cutting through the excited murmur of the crowd.

"Ladies and gentlemen, boys and girls of Tannenbaum Falls! It's my great pleasure to introduce two very special people who have captured the hearts of our town faster than Santa's reindeer on Christmas Eve!"

Merry's grip on Klaus's hand tightened as the emcee continued.

"First, we have the delightful Merry North, who has breathed new life into her grandmother's beloved bakery, keeping our bellies full and our spirits high with her heavenly Christmas cookies!"

A wave of applause and cheers erupted from the other side of the curtain, and Merry felt a rush of affection for the townsfolk she'd come to love.

"And joining her, the mysterious and talented Klaus Krampus, whose exquisite wooden toys have brought joy to children and adults alike, reminding us all of the magic of the season!"

Another round of enthusiastic clapping filled the air. Merry glanced up at Klaus, noticing a flicker of emotion in his eyes – was it pride? Nostalgia? She couldn't quite place it.

"Together," the emcee's voice swelled with emotion, "these two have shown us the true meaning of Christmas spirit, working tirelessly to preserve our cherished traditions and bring our community closer than ever before!"

As the applause reached a crescendo, Merry took a deep breath, her heart racing with a mixture of excitement and nerves. She felt Klaus squeeze her hand gently, and in that moment, she knew that whatever came next, they would face it together.

Merry's eyes locked with Klaus's, finding strength in his steady gaze. With a shared nod, they stepped onto the stage, hand in hand. The crowd's applause swelled, washing over them like a wave of warmth and acceptance.

Twinkling lights adorned the town square, casting a soft glow on the sea of familiar faces before them. Merry's heart swelled with emotion as she took in the sight of friends, neighbors, and customers, all beaming up at her and Klaus.

Taking a deep breath, Merry stepped forward to the microphone. Her voice, tinged with a slight tremor of excitement, rang out clear and sincere.

"Oh my goodness, I can't tell you how overwhelmed I am right now," she began, her green eyes sparkling. "When I first came to Tannenbaum Falls, I was just hoping to keep my grandmother's legacy alive. But what I've found here is so much more than I ever dreamed possible."

She paused, her gaze sweeping over the crowd. "You've welcomed me with open arms, shared your stories, your traditions, and your love for this wonderful town. And in doing so, you've reaffirmed something I've always believed in my heart – the incredible power of love and togetherness."

As she spoke, Merry felt Klaus's presence beside her, solid and reassuring. She thought of all the moments they'd shared over the past weeks – the late nights at the bakery, the laughter-filled toy-making sessions, the quiet walks through the snow-covered streets. Each memory was a testament to the connection they'd forged, not just with each other, but with the entire community.

"Every cookie baked, every smile shared, every act of kindness I've witnessed here has shown me that when we come together, there's nothing we can't accomplish," Merry continued, her voice growing stronger with each word. "You've all become my family, and I'm so grateful to be a part of this magical place."

Klaus gently took Merry's hand, his fingers intertwining with hers as he stepped forward. The warmth of his touch sent a flutter through her heart, and she watched as he addressed the crowd, his deep voice resonating with emotion.

"Friends and neighbors," Klaus began, his eyes glinting with centuries of wisdom, "I stand before you not just as a toymaker, but as someone who has witnessed the power of tradition firsthand." He squeezed Merry's hand, drawing strength from her presence. "Millie's bakery isn't just a place that serves delicious cookies. It's a beacon of joy, a cornerstone of what makes Tannenbaum Falls special."

Merry felt a lump form in her throat as Klaus continued, his words painting a vivid picture of her grandmother's legacy.

"Each recipe passed down, each batch of cookies lovingly prepared, carries with it the essence of our community's spirit. It's more than sugar and flour – it's the laughter of children, the warmth of family gatherings, the comfort of cherished memories."

As Klaus spoke, Merry glanced out at the sea of faces before them. She saw Mrs. Henderson, the town librarian, dabbing at her eyes with a handkerchief. Next to her, little Timmy Wilson was listening with rapt attention, his eyes wide with wonder.

"In preserving Millie's legacy," Klaus said, his voice growing softer, more intimate, "we're not just saving a bakery. We're safeguarding the very heart of Tannenbaum Falls. We're ensuring that the love, the togetherness, the magic that Millie poured into every cookie continues to touch lives for generations to come."

Merry felt tears prick at her own eyes, overwhelmed by the depth of Klaus's words and the palpable emotion emanating from the crowd. She thought of her grandmother, imagining how proud Millie would be to see her beloved town coming together like this.

As their speeches drew to a close, Merry turned to Klaus, her bright green eyes meeting his deep, wise gaze. In that moment, time seemed to stand still. The bustling crowd faded away, and it was just the two of them, sharing a silent conversation that spoke volumes.

Merry's heart swelled with emotion. She saw in Klaus's eyes a reflection of her own feelings – love, commitment, and a shared passion for this quaint town that had brought them together. A soft smile played on her lips as she thought, "We really are in this together, aren't we?"

Klaus's lips quirked up in response, as if he'd heard her unspoken words. His hand gave hers a gentle squeeze, conveying strength and support.

Suddenly, the spell was broken by a thunderous eruption of applause. Merry blinked, momentarily startled by the outpouring of enthusiasm from the crowd.

"Oh my," she whispered, her cheeks flushing with a mix of embarrassment and joy.

Klaus leaned in close, his breath warm against her ear. "I think they approve," he murmured, a hint of amusement in his voice.

Merry laughed, the sound bubbling up from deep within her. "I'd say that's an understatement," she replied, her eyes scanning the crowd.

She saw Mrs. Henderson on her feet, clapping vigorously. Little Timmy was jumping up and down, his face split by a wide grin. Even grumpy old Mr. Petersson, who'd initially been skeptical about the changes to Millie's bakery, was nodding approvingly.

"I never imagined..." Merry started, her voice thick with emotion.

"That we'd win them over so completely?" Klaus finished for her, his eyes twinkling. "My dear Merry, how could they not fall in love with you – with us – and everything we stand for?"

## A Very Krampus Christmas

As Merry and Klaus descended the stage steps, their hands remained firmly clasped. The warmth of Klaus's palm against hers sent a comforting tingle up Merry's arm. They had barely reached the bottom when a tidal wave of well-wishers engulfed them.

"Oh, Merry! Klaus! That was simply wonderful!" Mrs. Henderson exclaimed, her eyes brimming with tears of joy.

Merry found herself swept into a tight embrace by the older woman. "Thank you, Mrs. Henderson," she managed, her voice muffled against the woman's festive sweater.

"You two are just what this town needed," Mr. Petersson chimed in, his gruff voice softened by genuine emotion.

Klaus inclined his head graciously. "We're honored to be a part of Tannenbaum Falls," he replied, his old-world charm shining through.

Little Timmy pushed his way to the front, his eyes wide with excitement. "Ms. Merry, Mr. Klaus, will you make special cookies for Santa this year?"

Merry knelt down, her green eyes twinkling. "Of course, Timmy. We'll make the best cookies Santa's ever tasted."

As the crowd pressed closer, showering them with congratulations and questions about future plans for the bakery, Merry felt a gentle tug on her hand. She looked up to see Klaus gesturing subtly towards a quiet corner of the room.

"Excuse us for just a moment," Klaus said to the gathering, his voice polite but firm.

They made their way to the secluded spot, the sounds of the celebration fading to a gentle hum. Merry took a deep breath, savoring the moment of calm.

"Are you alright?" Klaus asked, his brow furrowed with concern.

Merry nodded, a soft smile playing on her lips. "More than alright. I'm just... overwhelmed. In the best possible way."

Klaus's expression softened. "Merry," he began, his voice low and intense, "I want you to know that I'm committed to this. To us. To preserving everything your grandmother built."

Merry felt her heart swell. "Oh, Klaus," she whispered, "I feel the same way. Millie's legacy, this town's traditions – they're a part of me now. A part of us."

"Together, then?" Klaus asked, extending his hand.

"Together," Merry agreed, placing her hand in his. As their fingers intertwined, she couldn't help but think how perfectly they fit – just like the pieces of a Christmas puzzle coming together at last.

As they rejoined the festivities, the lively strains of "Jingle Bell Rock" filled the air. Merry's eyes lit up, and she tugged gently on Klaus's hand.
"Oh, Klaus! I love this song. Dance with me?" she asked, her green eyes sparkling with excitement.
Klaus hesitated for a moment, his usual composure wavering. "I'm not much of a dancer, I'm afraid," he admitted, a hint of embarrassment coloring his cheeks.
Merry laughed, the sound as warm and inviting as freshly baked cookies. "Neither am I, but that's half the fun! Come on, I'll show you."
She led him onto the makeshift dance floor, where couples were already twirling and swaying. Merry placed one hand on Klaus's shoulder, guiding his other to her waist. As they began to move, she couldn't help but notice how natural it felt to be in his arms.
"See? You're doing great," she encouraged, beaming up at him.
Klaus chuckled, his initial stiffness melting away. "I suppose I had a good teacher," he replied, his eyes twinkling with affection.
As they danced, Merry noticed the joy radiating from the faces around them. Mrs. Claus, the town's beloved librarian, winked at her as she waltzed by with her husband. The Henderson twins, usually so mischievous, were helping to hang more twinkling lights, their faces alight with the spirit of the season.
"Look at everyone," Merry whispered to Klaus. "It's like the whole town is glowing."
Klaus nodded, his gaze warm as he surveyed the room. "It's not just the decorations," he observed. "There's a special kind of magic here tonight. Can you feel it?"
Merry's heart swelled with happiness. "I do," she replied softly. "It's in every smile, every laugh. It's like... like..."
"Like Christmas come to life," Klaus finished for her, pulling her a little closer as they swayed to the music.
As the lively music faded into a soft, melodic tune, Merry and Klaus found themselves drifting away from the center of the festivities.

They made their way to a quiet corner of the town square, where the twinkling lights cast a warm glow on the freshly fallen snow.

Merry leaned against the old oak tree, its branches adorned with sparkling icicles. She gazed up at Klaus, her green eyes reflecting the shimmer of the lights. "Can you believe how far we've come?" she asked, her voice soft with wonder.

Klaus took her hand, his touch gentle yet reassuring. "It's been quite the journey, hasn't it?" he replied, a hint of his old-world charm coloring his words. "From strangers to... this."

Merry laughed softly, squeezing his hand. "I never imagined when I came to Tannenbaum Falls that I'd find... well, you."

"Nor did I expect to find someone who could see beyond my gruff exterior," Klaus admitted, his eyes twinkling with mirth. "You've taught me so much about embracing change, Merry."

She tilted her head, curiosity piqued. "Oh? And what have you learned, Mr. Krampus?"

"That sometimes, the best traditions are the ones we create together," he said, pulling her closer. "And that a little cookie magic can warm even the coldest of hearts."

Merry's laughter rang out, clear and bright in the crisp night air. As it subsided, she looked around at the town square, filled with the joy and warmth of their friends and neighbors. "We couldn't have done this without them," she murmured, feeling a wave of gratitude wash over her.

Klaus nodded, his gaze following hers. "Their support has been invaluable. It's as if the entire town conspired to bring us together."

As the night drew to a close, the crowd began to thin, leaving behind a peaceful silence punctuated only by the soft tinkling of distant bells. Merry and Klaus found themselves standing beneath an archway draped in mistletoe and twinkling lights.

Klaus cupped Merry's face gently, his eyes full of love and promise. "Merry North," he said, his voice low and tender, "you've brought more joy to my life than I thought possible."

Merry's heart raced as she leaned into his touch. "And you, Klaus Krampus, have shown me the true magic of Christmas."

As their lips met in a sweet, tender kiss, Merry knew that their story – a tale of love, tradition, and the spirit of Christmas – would forever be woven into the fabric of Tannenbaum Falls.

As they broke apart from their kiss, Merry's eyes sparkled with joy and unshed tears. She gazed up at Klaus, marveling at how his usually enigmatic features now radiated warmth and contentment.

"You know," Merry said, her voice soft and playful, "I never thought I'd fall in love with the Toymaker of Tannenbaum Falls."

Klaus chuckled, the sound rich and deep. "And I never imagined a baker would capture my heart with sugar cookies and determination."

They turned to face the town square, Klaus's arm draped comfortably around Merry's shoulders. The last of the festival-goers were saying their goodbyes, their voices filled with cheer and promise of future gatherings.

Merry leaned into Klaus, inhaling the scent of pine and cinnamon that seemed to follow him everywhere. "What do you think the future holds for us, Klaus?"

He smiled, his eyes twinkling with centuries-old wisdom and newfound hope. "I believe, my dear Merry, that our future is as bright as the star atop the town's Christmas tree. Full of love, laughter, and more gingerbread than even I can eat."

Merry giggled, picturing Klaus surrounded by mountains of her grandmother's famous gingerbread. "And traditions," she added. "Old and new."

"Indeed," Klaus agreed, giving her a gentle squeeze. "We'll keep the spirit of Christmas alive in Tannenbaum Falls, one cookie and handcrafted toy at a time."

As they stood there, basking in the glow of their love and the twinkling lights, Merry felt a sense of belonging she'd never experienced before. This town, with its quirky traditions and warm-hearted people, had become more than just a home. It was the setting for their own personal Christmas miracle.

# Chapter 16

Merry's hand felt warm and secure in Klaus's as they strolled through the twinkling lights of Tannenbaum Falls' town square. The air was crisp with the scent of pine and cinnamon, and the cheerful chatter of townspeople filled her ears. She couldn't help but smile, feeling a sense of belonging she'd never experienced before.

"I must say, Ms. North," Klaus said with a twinkle in his eye, "your grandmother would be proud of how you've brought this festival to life."

Merry laughed, a sound as light and joyful as sleigh bells. "I couldn't have done it without you, Mr. Krampus. Your toy-making skills are truly magical."

As they passed by the hot chocolate stand, the rich aroma wafting through the air, Merry's thoughts drifted to how much her life had changed in just a few short weeks. She'd come to Tannenbaum Falls feeling lost, but now...

Her reverie was interrupted by a familiar, mischievous voice. "Miss Merry! Mr. Klaus!"

Merry turned to see Tommy Jenkins bounding towards them, his blond hair sticking up in all directions and his cheeks flushed with excitement. She couldn't help but grin at the sight of him.

"Well, if it isn't our little troublemaker," Klaus said, his stern tone belied by the warmth in his eyes.

Tommy skidded to a stop in front of them, slightly out of breath. "I made something for you, Miss Merry," he said, holding out a small package wrapped in newspaper.

Merry's heart swelled with emotion as she carefully unwrapped the gift. Inside was a handmade ornament - a perfectly imperfect gingerbread man, crafted from clay and painted with careful, if slightly wobbly, strokes.

"Oh, Tommy," she breathed, her eyes misting over. "It's beautiful."

Tommy beamed, his freckles dancing across his cheeks. "It's to say thanks for saving the festival. And for teaching me how to make cookies without burning down the kitchen."

Merry laughed, remembering the near-disaster of their baking lesson. She knelt down to Tommy's level, ornament clutched carefully in her hand. "Thank you, Tommy. This means more to me than you know."

As she hugged the young boy, Merry caught Klaus's eye over Tommy's shoulder. The tenderness in his gaze made her heart skip a beat. In that moment, surrounded by the festive cheer of the town square and the love of her new community, Merry knew she was exactly where she was meant to be.

The lively strains of "Jingle Bell Rock" filled the air, and Merry felt her feet begin to tap of their own accord. She glanced at Klaus, a mischievous glint in her green eyes.

"Care to show these folks how it's done, Mr. Krampus?" she asked, extending her hand.

Klaus raised an eyebrow, his lips quirking into a half-smile. "I'm not sure centuries-old spirits are known for their dancing prowess, Miss North."

Despite his protest, he took her hand, and Merry's heart fluttered at the warmth of his touch. She led him towards the giant Christmas tree at the center of the square, where couples and families were already twirling and laughing.

"Just follow my lead," Merry said, placing one hand on Klaus's shoulder and guiding his to her waist.

As they began to move, Merry was pleasantly surprised by Klaus's natural grace. His old-world charm translated into elegant, measured steps that perfectly complemented her more exuberant style.

"You've been holding out on me," she teased, her cheeks flushed with exertion and joy.

Klaus spun her gently, his dark eyes twinkling. "A man must have some secrets, my dear."

As they danced, Merry couldn't help but marvel at the scene around them. The townspeople of Tannenbaum Falls, once wary and divided, now moved as one vibrant, joyous entity. Children darted between the legs of adults, tinsel trailing from their mittened hands. Elderly couples swayed together, reliving memories of festivals past.

"We did it," Merry whispered, more to herself than to Klaus. "We really brought them together."

Before Klaus could respond, a familiar voice cut through the music. "Miss North? Might I have a word?"

Merry turned to see Mayor Harlow standing nearby, his usual air of pompous authority notably diminished. She exchanged a quick glance with Klaus before stepping away from their dance.

"Of course, Mayor," she said, trying to keep the apprehension from her voice. What now?

The mayor cleared his throat, clearly uncomfortable. "I... I owe you an apology, Miss North. I was short-sighted in my opposition to this festival. Seeing our community come together like this... well, it's a testament to the importance of our traditions. And to your dedication in preserving them."

Merry blinked, stunned by the unexpected turn of events. She felt Klaus's reassuring presence at her back as she formulated a response.

"Thank you, Mayor Harlow," she said finally, a warm smile spreading across her face. "That means a great deal to me. And to the memory of my grandmother."

The mayor nodded, a hint of his old bluster returning. "Yes, well, you can count on my full support for future events. Tannenbaum Falls will continue to be a beacon of holiday spirit, thanks in no small part to your efforts."

As Mayor Harlow moved away, Merry turned to Klaus, her eyes shining with unshed tears of joy. "Did you hear that? We did it. We really, truly did it."

Klaus pulled her close, his strong arms enveloping her in a warm embrace. "We did, my dear. And I have a feeling this is just the beginning of something wonderful."

The brass bell above the door chimed merrily as Merry and Klaus stepped into Millie's bakery. A wave of warmth and the heavenly aroma of cinnamon and vanilla washed over them, instantly transporting Merry back to her childhood. She inhaled deeply, savoring the familiar scents.

"Oh, Klaus," she breathed, her eyes taking in the twinkling lights and garlands adorning every surface. "It's just like I remember it."

Klaus squeezed her hand gently. "Your grandmother's spirit is alive in every corner," he observed, his gaze soft as he watched Merry's reaction.

Merry moved towards the display case, her fingers trailing along the polished wood. "Look," she said, pointing to a faded photograph tucked into the corner of the frame. "That's Millie on her first day of business."

Klaus leaned in, studying the image of a young woman with Merry's same vibrant smile. "She looks so proud," he murmured.

"She was," Merry replied, her voice thick with emotion. "This bakery was her dream. And now..."

"And now it's yours," Klaus finished, turning to face her. His blue eyes held a depth of understanding that made Merry's heart skip a beat.

She took a deep breath, the scent of freshly baked cookies filling her lungs. "Klaus, I... I think I want to stay. To run the bakery full-time. To keep Millie's legacy alive."

Klaus's face broke into a radiant smile. "I was hoping you'd say that," he admitted. "Tannenbaum Falls needs you, Merry. And I... well, I need you too."

Merry felt a rush of warmth that had nothing to do with the ovens. "You do?"

"More than I ever thought possible," Klaus said softly. "This town, this bakery – they're a part of you. And I want to be a part of it all too, if you'll have me."

Merry's heart soared. She reached out, taking both of Klaus's hands in hers. "There's nothing I want more," she whispered, her eyes shining with unshed tears of joy.

As they stood there, surrounded by the warmth and memories of Millie's bakery, Merry felt a sense of rightness settle over her. This was where she belonged – carrying on her grandmother's legacy, building a future with Klaus, and keeping the spirit of Christmas alive in Tannenbaum Falls.

Merry's heart raced as she stepped onto the small stage in the town square, her hand clasped tightly in Klaus's. The twinkling lights of the Christmas tree cast a warm glow over the gathered crowd, their faces expectant and curious.

"Everyone," Merry called out, her voice wavering slightly with nerves and excitement. "Klaus and I have an announcement to make."

The crowd hushed, and Merry felt Klaus squeeze her hand reassuringly. She took a deep breath, drawing strength from his presence.

"We've decided to stay in Tannenbaum Falls," she continued, her green eyes sparkling. "We're going to run Millie's bakery full-time and keep her legacy alive."

A beat of silence, then the square erupted in cheers and applause. Merry's eyes welled up with tears as she saw the genuine joy on the faces of her new neighbors and friends.

"You've all made us feel so welcome," Klaus added, his deep voice carrying over the crowd. "We couldn't imagine calling anywhere else home."

As they stepped down from the stage, they were engulfed in a sea of well-wishers. Merry found herself swept up in hugs and congratulations, her heart overflowing with warmth.

"Oh, thank goodness," Mrs. Pendleton, the town librarian, exclaimed. "I was worried we'd lose the best gingerbread in the state!"

Merry laughed, feeling a surge of affection for this quirky, tight-knit community. As she made her way through the crowd, she caught sight of a sprig of mistletoe hanging from a nearby lamppost. Her eyes met Klaus's, and a spark of mischief danced between them.

With a playful smile, Merry tugged Klaus towards the mistletoe. As they stood beneath it, the noise of the crowd seemed to fade away. Klaus cupped her face gently, his touch sending shivers down her spine.

"Merry North," he murmured, his eyes filled with love and promise, "you've brought more joy to my life than I thought possible."

"And you've shown me the true meaning of home," Merry whispered back.

Their lips met in a kiss that was both tender and passionate, sealing their commitment to each other and to their new life in Tannenbaum Falls. As they parted, Merry's cheeks flushed with happiness, she thought, 'This is it. This is where I belong.'

The townspeople's cheers and wolf-whistles brought them back to reality, and Merry buried her face in Klaus's chest, laughing with embarrassment and pure, unbridled joy.

The town hall bustled with activity as Merry and Klaus made their way to the grand feast. The aroma of cinnamon, nutmeg, and freshly baked cookies filled the air, reminiscent of Millie's bakery in its heyday. Merry's heart swelled with pride as she saw trays upon trays of her grandmother's famous Christmas cookies adorning the tables.

"I can't believe we pulled this off," Merry whispered to Klaus, squeezing his hand.

Klaus smiled warmly, his eyes twinkling. "With your determination and this town's spirit, I never doubted it for a moment."

They settled into their seats, surrounded by the cheerful chatter of their neighbors. Mrs. Pendleton leaned over, her eyes sparkling with mischief. "You two make such a lovely couple. When's the wedding?"

Merry nearly choked on her hot cocoa, feeling her cheeks flush. "Oh, we haven't... I mean, we're not..."

Klaus chuckled, coming to her rescue. "We're taking things one cookie at a time, Mrs. Pendleton."

As laughter rippled through their corner of the table, Merry found herself gazing at the faces around her. Each one held a story, a connection to this place she now called home. Her eyes landed on a plate of gingerbread men, decorated just as her grandmother had always done.

Picking one up, she took a bite and closed her eyes, savoring the familiar taste. In that moment, she could almost hear Millie's gentle voice: "Remember, dear, it's not just about the recipe. It's about the love you bake into every cookie."

Merry opened her eyes, feeling a wave of emotion wash over her. "You know," she said softly to Klaus, "when I first came here, I thought I was just saving a bakery. But really, Tannenbaum Falls saved me."

Klaus wrapped an arm around her shoulders, pulling her close. "And in doing so, you've saved a little bit of Christmas magic for all of us."

As the feast continued around them, Merry took a moment to truly absorb the scene. The laughter, the warmth, the sense of belonging – it was everything she had ever wanted and more. She thought to herself, 'Grandma Millie, I hope you can see this. Your legacy lives on, and it's more beautiful than I ever imagined.'

As the final crumbs of Millie's cookies were savored, Merry stood up, her green eyes twinkling with inspiration. She reached for Klaus's hand, giving it a gentle squeeze.

## A Very Krampus Christmas

"Everyone," she called out, her voice warm and inviting, "I think it's time we wrap up this wonderful evening with a song. What do you say?"

Klaus nodded, a rare smile spreading across his usually enigmatic features. "An excellent idea, my dear. Music has a way of binding hearts together."

The townspeople gathered around, their faces alight with anticipation. Merry took a deep breath, her auburn hair catching the glow of the nearby Christmas lights.

"Let's sing 'Silent Night,'" she suggested, her voice soft but carrying. "It was Grandma Millie's favorite."

As Merry and Klaus began to sing, their voices blended in perfect harmony. Klaus's deep, rich tone complemented Merry's clear, sweet melody. One by one, the townsfolk joined in, their voices rising and falling like gentle waves.

Merry felt a lump form in her throat as she sang, overwhelmed by the sense of unity surrounding her. She thought, 'This is what community feels like. This is what Grandma Millie always wanted for me.'

As the last notes faded away, Merry looked at Klaus, her eyes shining with unshed tears. He squeezed her hand, understanding without words the depth of her emotion.

"Thank you all," Merry said, her voice slightly husky. "For everything. For making Tannenbaum Falls feel like home."

Klaus cleared his throat, his usually measured tone tinged with warmth. "Indeed. You've shown us the true spirit of Christmas – love, belonging, and the power of tradition."

As the gathering began to disperse, Merry's mind drifted to the future. She could see herself and Klaus, years from now, still in this charming town. The bakery would be thriving, filled with the scent of Millie's famous cookies and the laughter of children. They'd be surrounded by friends who had become family, continuing the traditions that made Tannenbaum Falls so special.

She turned to Klaus, a soft smile playing on her lips. "What do you think, Mr. Krampus? Ready for a lifetime of Christmas magic?"

Klaus's eyes twinkled with centuries-old wisdom and newfound love. "With you, my dear Merry, every day will be magical."

# Chapter 17

Merry North sank deeper into the plush armchair, her grandmother's cherished quilt draped over her lap. The living room of her childhood summers—now her own home—embraced her like a warm hug. As the fire crackled in the hearth, casting dancing shadows on the walls, Merry's gaze drifted to the twinkling Christmas lights still adorning the room.

"Oh, Gran," she whispered, a bittersweet smile tugging at her lips. "I hope I'm doing you proud."

The scent of cinnamon and pine mingled in the air, a comforting reminder of holidays past. Merry closed her eyes, drinking in the cozy atmosphere. The soft glow of the lights reflected off the polished ornaments on the mantel, creating a magical ambiance that seemed to whisper of new beginnings.

Merry's fingers absently traced the intricate patterns on the quilt. "I never thought I'd be back here, running the bakery," she mused aloud. "But it feels right, doesn't it?"

The gentle pop of the fire seemed to answer in agreement. Merry chuckled softly, shaking her head at her own whimsy. Her eyes landed on a framed photo of her grandmother, smiling brightly from behind the bakery counter.

"I miss you, Gran," Merry said, her voice thick with emotion. "But I feel you here with me, guiding me through this new chapter."

She reached for her mug of hot cocoa, letting the warmth seep into her hands. The marshmallows had long since melted, leaving a sweet froth on top. As she sipped, Merry's gaze wandered around the room, taking in the familiar knick-knacks and treasured mementos that now belonged to her.

"Who would have thought," she murmured, "that coming back to Tannenbaum Falls would feel so much like coming home?"

The quiet of the room was broken only by the steady tick of the antique clock on the mantel and the occasional snap of the fire. Merry pulled the quilt tighter around her shoulders, feeling a deep sense of contentment settle over her.

"I think I'm exactly where I'm meant to be," she said softly, raising her mug in a silent toast to her grandmother and the journey that had brought her back to this cherished place.

Merry's eyes drifted to the window, where a light dusting of snow was falling, and her mind wandered back to the Tannenbaum Falls Winter Festival. A warm smile spread across her face as she remembered the twinkling lights, the sound of carols, and the laughter that had filled the town square.

"Oh, what a night that was," she said aloud, her voice full of fondness. "I've never seen the town so alive."

She closed her eyes, recalling the moment she'd stepped onto the stage to light the town Christmas tree. The crowd's cheers had washed over her, filling her heart with an overwhelming sense of belonging.

"I felt like I was truly part of something special," Merry mused, her fingers absently tracing the pattern on her mug. "Like I'd found my place in this wonderful, quirky little town."

A chuckle escaped her as she remembered Mayor Frostwell's elaborate speech, complete with his trademark puns. "Who knew the 'yule log' could be used in so many jokes?"

Her laughter faded into a contented sigh as she reflected on the challenges she'd faced since arriving in Tannenbaum Falls. The bakery had seemed like an insurmountable task at first, with its outdated equipment and dwindling customer base.

"There were days I thought I'd made a huge mistake," Merry admitted to herself, shaking her head. "But look at us now, Gran. We did it."

She remembered the day she'd finally mastered her grandmother's famous gingerbread recipe, after countless failed attempts. The smell of spices had filled the bakery, and when she'd taken that first bite, tears had sprung to her eyes.

"It was like you were there with me," Merry whispered, her voice catching. "Guiding my hands, just like when I was little."

As if on cue, a fresh wave of heavenly aroma wafted through the air, pulling Merry from her reverie. The unmistakable scent of cinnamon, nutmeg, and vanilla danced around her, wrapping her in a comforting embrace.

"Oh, the cookies!" Merry exclaimed, jumping to her feet. She hurried to the kitchen, her sock-clad feet padding softly on the worn wooden floor.

Opening the oven door, she was greeted by a rush of warm, fragrant air. The sight of perfectly golden-brown sugar cookies brought a wide smile to her face. As she carefully removed the tray, Merry felt a swell of pride and contentment.

"Gran would be so proud," she murmured, setting the tray on the cooling rack. "Running this bakery... it's more than just a job. It's like keeping a piece of her alive."

The doorbell chimed, interrupting her thoughts. Merry wiped her hands on her apron and went to answer it, finding Mrs. Tinsel, her neighbor, on the doorstep.

"Merry, dear! I couldn't help but smell those delightful cookies of yours," Mrs. Tinsel said, her eyes twinkling. "I thought I'd pop by and say hello."

Merry beamed, ushering her in. "Perfect timing! They're just out of the oven. Would you like to try one?"

As they settled in the kitchen, Merry couldn't help but reflect on the warmth of the community. "You know, Mrs. Tinsel, I never expected to form such wonderful friendships when I first arrived here."

Mrs. Tinsel patted her hand. "Oh, honey, that's what Tannenbaum Falls is all about. We take care of our own."

Merry nodded, her eyes drifting to the window where snow was gently falling. Her thoughts turned to Klaus, and a soft smile played on her lips.

"You've got that look again," Mrs. Tinsel said, her eyes twinkling. "Thinking about that handsome toymaker of yours?"

Merry felt a blush creep up her cheeks. "Is it that obvious?"

"Only to someone who's seen true love before," Mrs. Tinsel chuckled. "Tell me, dear, what is it about Klaus that makes your eyes light up like that?"

Merry's fingers traced the rim of her mug as she considered the question. "It's... everything," she said softly. "The way he listens, really listens. How he can make me laugh even on the toughest days. And there's this... depth to him. Like he understands things beyond what most people see."

She paused, remembering their walk in the snow last week, how Klaus had pointed out the intricate patterns of frost on the trees. "He sees beauty in the smallest things, Mrs. Tinsel. It's like he's lived a hundred lifetimes, yet he's still filled with wonder."

Mrs. Tinsel nodded knowingly. "That's a rare gift, dear. You two have something special."

Merry's gaze swept across the bakery, taking in the warm glow of the lights, the familiar scent of vanilla and cinnamon. "You know, when I first came here, I thought running the bakery would be a burden. But now..." She shook her head, smiling. "It's become my passion. My home."

"And we're all the better for it," Mrs. Tinsel said, raising her mug in a small toast. "To finding your place, Merry. May your days be merry and bright."

Merry clinked her mug against Mrs. Tinsel's, feeling a wave of gratitude wash over her. She had found more than just a bakery in Tannenbaum Falls. She had found her heart's true home.

The soft strains of "Have Yourself a Merry Little Christmas" drifted through the living room, mingling with the crackling of the fire. Merry hummed along, her fingers absently tracing the rim of her mug as she gazed out the frost-kissed window.

"You know," she said aloud, though she was alone, "I never thought I'd be one of those people who talks to themselves."

She chuckled softly, the sound merging with the melody. The music seemed to wrap around her like a warm blanket, enhancing the cozy atmosphere and stirring memories of Christmases past and present.

Merry's eyes drifted to a framed photo on the mantel - her and Klaus at the town's tree lighting ceremony. His enigmatic smile, the way his eyes crinkled at the corners, sent a flutter through her chest.

"I wonder what you're doing right now," she mused, picturing Klaus in his workshop, carefully crafting another intricate wooden toy.

She closed her eyes, allowing herself to imagine a future here in Tannenbaum Falls. The bakery thriving, filled with the laughter of children and the chatter of neighbors. Klaus by her side, his steady presence a constant source of strength and wonder.

"It's funny," Merry said softly, opening her eyes. "I came here thinking it was temporary, but now..." She trailed off, a smile playing on her lips. "Now I can't imagine being anywhere else."

The music swelled, and Merry found herself standing, swaying gently to the rhythm. She spun slowly, taking in the room that had become so dear to her.

"I think Grandma would be proud," she whispered, her heart full of peace and possibility.

Merry's eyes misted over as she gazed around the cozy living room, her heart swelling with gratitude. She picked up a framed photo of the town's festival, her fingers tracing the smiling faces of her new friends and neighbors.

"I never expected to find this," she murmured, her voice thick with emotion. "Such love, such acceptance."

She set the photo down and walked to the window, watching the gentle snowfall outside. The twinkling lights of Main Street glowed in the distance, a beacon of warmth in the winter night.

"You know," Merry said, addressing the room as if her grandmother's spirit still lingered, "when I first arrived, I was so afraid of disappointing everyone. But they've all been so supportive, so patient."

She turned back to the room, a soft smile playing on her lips. "Mrs. Claus – I mean, Edna – has been like a second grandmother to me. And Tom at the hardware store always has a kind word and a discount for the bakery."

Merry's eyes lit up as she continued, "And don't even get me started on Klaus. He's been... well, he's been my rock through all of this."

She walked over to the kitchen, the scent of cinnamon and vanilla still lingering in the air. Running her hand along the well-worn countertop, Merry felt a renewed sense of purpose course through her.

"I think I finally understand, Grandma," she said, her voice filled with determination. "This isn't just about keeping the bakery going. It's about preserving a piece of Tannenbaum Falls' heart."

Merry squared her shoulders, a look of resolve settling on her face. "I'm ready for this. For all of it. The challenges, the joys, the endless batches of snickerdoodles," she chuckled.

As she began gathering ingredients for tomorrow's baking, Merry felt a sense of excitement bubbling up inside her. "Watch out,

## A Very Krampus Christmas

Tannenbaum Falls," she said with a grin, "Merry North is here to stay, and she's got some big plans for this little bakery."

## Chapter 18

Merry's eyes fluttered open as the sound of distant laughter tickled her ears. She blinked away the remnants of sleep, her lips curving into a soft smile as realization dawned. Christmas morning had arrived in Tannenbaum Falls.

She turned to find Klaus already awake, his deep blue eyes twinkling with childlike excitement. "Merry Christmas, my love," he whispered, his voice warm and rich like hot cocoa on a winter's night.

"Merry Christmas, Klaus," she replied, snuggling closer to him. The warmth of his embrace enveloped her, and she breathed in his familiar scent of pine and cinnamon.

Klaus chuckled, the sound rumbling through his chest. "I do believe I hear the dulcet tones of your nieces and nephews downstairs. They seem rather eager to begin the day's festivities."

Merry grinned, her green eyes sparkling. "I'm surprised they haven't stormed our bedroom yet. Remember last year?"

"Ah yes, the Great Christmas Morning Ambush of 2022," Klaus said with mock solemnity. "How could I forget?"

Merry giggled, planting a quick kiss on his cheek before reluctantly pulling away from his embrace. "We'd better head down before they come looking for us. I can practically feel their impatience from here."

As they rose from the bed, Merry couldn't help but marvel at how natural this all felt – waking up beside Klaus on Christmas morning, their families gathered downstairs, the promise of a day filled with love and laughter stretching out before them.

"What are you thinking about?" Klaus asked softly, his hand finding hers as they made their way to the bedroom door.

## A Very Krampus Christmas

Merry squeezed his fingers, her heart swelling with affection. "Just how perfect this is. How perfect you are. How did I get so lucky?"

Klaus's eyes softened, and he brought her hand to his lips, pressing a gentle kiss to her knuckles. "My dear Merry, I believe I'm the lucky one. You've brought more joy to my life than I thought possible in all my centuries."

As they stepped out into the hallway, the sounds of excitement grew louder. Merry could hear her mother's laughter mingling with the delighted squeals of children, and the deep, booming voice of Klaus's father regaling someone with what was undoubtedly a centuries-old Christmas tale.

"Ready to face the chaos?" Merry asked, her eyes twinkling with mischief.

Klaus straightened his shoulders, a playful smirk tugging at his lips. "My dear, I've faced down Krampus himself. I think I can handle a few excited children on Christmas morning."

Hand in hand, they descended the stairs, ready to embrace the magic and mayhem of Christmas in Tannenbaum Falls.

The kitchen was a scene of festive chaos as Merry and Klaus entered, hand in hand. Sunlight streamed through the frosted windows, casting a warm glow on the snow-dusted evergreens outside. Merry's eyes lit up at the sight of two crisp, red aprons hanging on the pantry door, each embroidered with their names in swirling gold thread.

"Oh, Klaus," she breathed, running her fingers over the delicate stitching. "When did you have time to make these?"

Klaus's eyes twinkled with mischief as he reached for the aprons. "A toymaker never reveals his secrets, my dear. But let's just say I had a little help from some industrious elves."

As they donned their matching aprons, Merry couldn't help but giggle at the sight of Klaus – the enigmatic Christmas spirit – looking so domestic. She reached up to smooth a stray lock of his dark hair, her touch lingering on his cheek.

"So, what shall we make for our Christmas feast?" Klaus asked, his voice warm with affection.

Merry's mind raced with possibilities. "Well, we can't forget Grandma's cinnamon rolls. And your father mentioned something about a centuries-old recipe for spiced hot chocolate?"

As they moved around the kitchen in perfect harmony, gathering ingredients and preheating the oven, Merry found herself marveling at how natural it all felt. She watched Klaus expertly measure out flour, his brow furrowed in concentration, and felt a surge of love so strong it nearly took her breath away.

"You know," she said, cracking eggs into a bowl, "if someone had told me last Christmas that I'd be spending this one with an actual Christmas spirit, I would have thought they'd had too much eggnog."

Klaus chuckled, the sound deep and rich. "And if someone had told me I'd find my heart's true home in a small town bakery, I might have sent them to have a stern talk with Krampus."

As the scent of cinnamon and vanilla filled the air, Merry couldn't help but reflect on their journey. "It's been quite the adventure, hasn't it? From you mysteriously appearing in my grandmother's bakery to saving Christmas for the whole town."

Klaus paused in his mixing, his eyes meeting hers with an intensity that made her heart skip. "Every moment has been a gift, Merry. You've taught me more about the true spirit of Christmas than I've learned in centuries."

Merry felt tears prick at her eyes, overwhelmed by the love and gratitude she felt. "Oh, Klaus," she whispered, flour-dusted hands reaching for him. "Tannenbaum Falls may be magical, but you're the real miracle in my life."

As their lips met in a tender kiss, Merry knew that no matter what challenges lay ahead, their love – born of cookie dough and Christmas magic – would see them through.

The aroma of freshly baked cinnamon rolls and sizzling bacon wafted through the air as Merry and Klaus carried platters of food to the dining room. Merry's heart swelled with joy at the sight of their families gathered around the table, faces bright with anticipation.

"Breakfast is served!" Merry announced, placing a tray of golden waffles in the center of the table.

Klaus followed, setting down a steaming pot of hot cocoa. "And what's Christmas morning without a little sweetness?" he added with a wink.

As everyone dug in, the room filled with the clinking of cutlery and happy chatter. Merry's mother, her eyes twinkling, leaned in conspiratorially. "So, Merry, dear, when can we expect some little elves running around?"

Merry nearly choked on her bite of waffle. "Mom!" she exclaimed, feeling her cheeks flush.

Klaus, ever the gentleman, smoothly interjected. "We're taking things one magical moment at a time, aren't we, my dear?" He squeezed Merry's hand under the table, and she felt a rush of gratitude for his tact.

As the meal progressed, stories flowed as freely as the maple syrup. Klaus regaled them with tales of Christmases past, carefully edited for mortal ears, while Merry's family shared embarrassing childhood anecdotes that had everyone in stitches.

When the last crumb had been savored, Merry stood up, her eyes sparkling with excitement. "I think it's time for another Christmas tradition, don't you?"

A chorus of eager agreement rose from the table. Klaus rose to join her, his voice warm with affection. "Lead the way, my Christmas cookie."

They guided their families to the living room, where a mountain of colorfully wrapped presents awaited. Merry couldn't help but notice how Klaus's eyes lit up, reminding her of his centuries as a toymaker.

"Youngest goes first!" Merry announced, handing a gift to her young nephew.

As paper tore and bows flew, the room filled with gasps of delight and heartfelt thank-yous. Merry's heart nearly burst with happiness as she watched Klaus carefully unwrap each gift, treating even the simplest present with reverence.

"Oh, Merry," he breathed, holding up a hand-knitted scarf. "It's perfect."

Merry leaned in, whispering, "I made it myself. I thought it might remind you of me when you're out spreading Christmas cheer."

Klaus's eyes shimmered with emotion. "My dear, everything reminds me of you. You've become the very essence of Christmas to me."

As they shared a tender kiss, Merry knew that this Christmas – and every one to come – would be filled with more magic than she'd ever dreamed possible.

With the last of the wrapping paper cleared away, Merry took Klaus's hand and led their families towards the grand Christmas tree that stood proudly in the corner of the living room. Its branches were laden with twinkling lights and an eclectic array of ornaments, each one telling a story of Christmases past.

"Oh, Klaus," Merry breathed, her green eyes wide with wonder. "Isn't it beautiful? Look at all these memories we've collected over the years."

Klaus nodded, his gaze softening as he took in the sight. "Indeed, my dear. Each bauble holds a piece of our hearts."

Merry reached out, gently touching a delicate glass snowflake. "This one was my grandmother's. She gave it to me the year I took over the bakery."

"And this," Klaus said, indicating a small wooden nutcracker, "I carved the first Christmas we spent together in Tannenbaum Falls."

As their families gathered around, Merry felt a warmth spreading through her chest. She thought about how far they'd come, from strangers to soulmates, all in the span of a magical holiday season.

"Shall we join hands?" Klaus suggested, his voice rich with emotion. "It's a tradition where I come from, to take a moment of reflection on this blessed day."

Merry nodded, reaching for her mother's hand on one side and Klaus's on the other. As the circle closed, she felt the energy of love and togetherness pulse through their joined hands.

"What are you thinking about, Klaus?" she asked softly, noticing the contemplative look on his face.

He smiled, his eyes twinkling like the lights on the tree. "I'm thinking about the true meaning of Christmas, my love. It's not about the presents or even the traditions, but about this – the love we share, the bonds we forge, and the joy we bring to others."

Merry felt tears prick at her eyes. "You're right. I'm so grateful for all of this, for everyone here, and especially for you, Klaus. You've brought so much magic into my life."

As they stood there, hand in hand, Merry realized that this moment – surrounded by family, love, and the spirit of Christmas – was the greatest gift of all.

The warmth of the moment lingered as Merry's eyes sparkled with excitement. "Who's ready to bake some cookies?" she asked, her voice brimming with enthusiasm.

## A Very Krampus Christmas

A chorus of eager responses filled the air as they made their way to the kitchen. Merry's heart swelled with joy as she watched Klaus tie on the 'Kiss the Cook' apron she'd gifted him earlier.

"Alright, troops," Klaus announced with a playful grin, "let's show these cookies who's boss!"

Merry chuckled, pulling out her grandmother's recipe box. "I think it's time we introduce you to the famous North family sugar cookie recipe," she said, running her fingers over the worn index card.

As they began mixing ingredients, flour dusted the air like a gentle snowfall. Merry couldn't help but smile as she watched Klaus meticulously roll out the dough, his brow furrowed in concentration.

"You know," she mused, cutting out a star-shaped cookie, "I never thought I'd see the day when the mysterious Klaus Krampus would be covered in flour and frosting."

Klaus looked up, a smudge of flour on his cheek. "Life is full of surprises, my dear. Much like this dough – moldable, full of potential, and sweetest when shared."

Merry's heart melted at his words. She thought to herself, 'How did I get so lucky?'

As they worked, the kitchen filled with laughter and the sweet aroma of baking cookies. Merry's mom regaled them with stories of Christmases past, while Klaus shared snippets of holiday traditions from around the world.

Soon, the first batch was in the oven, and Merry set the timer. "What do you say we bring a little music to this baking party?" she suggested, her eyes twinkling mischievously.

"Splendid idea!" Klaus exclaimed, wiping his hands on a towel. "I know just the carol to start with."

As Klaus began to sing 'Silent Night' in a rich baritone, Merry joined in, her clear soprano blending perfectly with his voice. One by one, their family members added their voices to the impromptu choir, creating a harmony that seemed to make the very walls of the kitchen resonate with Christmas spirit.

The timer chimed, and Merry pulled the last batch of cookies from the oven, their sweet aroma filling the kitchen. She set them on the cooling rack, admiring the golden-brown edges and festive shapes.

"They're perfect," Klaus said, his eyes twinkling with pride. He reached for a snowflake-shaped cookie, but Merry playfully swatted his hand away.

"Not yet, Mr. Krampus," she teased. "These are for our neighbors, remember?"

Klaus chuckled, his deep laugh warming Merry's heart. "Of course, my dear. Old habits die hard, I suppose."

Together, they began arranging the cooled cookies on an array of festive platters. Merry's mind wandered as she worked, thinking about how much her life had changed since meeting Klaus. 'Who would have thought I'd be spending Christmas with a centuries-old Christmas spirit?' she mused silently.

"Penny for your thoughts?" Klaus asked, noticing her contemplative expression.

Merry smiled, carefully placing a reindeer-shaped cookie on a platter. "Just thinking about how magical this all is. The bakery, you, this town... it feels like a dream."

Klaus gently took her hand, his touch sending a warm tingle through her. "It's very real, Merry. And it's only the beginning."

As they finished arranging the cookies, Merry's mother appeared with a stack of colorful tins. "For easier transport," she explained with a wink.

"Mom, you're a lifesaver!" Merry exclaimed, giving her a quick hug.

They worked efficiently, transferring the cookies into the tins and loading them into their cars. As Merry closed the trunk of her car, she turned to Klaus with a grin. "Ready for a Tannenbaum Falls Christmas adventure?"

Klaus offered his arm gallantly. "My dear, with you, I'm ready for anything."

Merry's heart swelled with joy as they approached Mrs. Finklestein's quaint cottage. The elderly woman's eyes lit up when she saw them coming up her snow-dusted path.

"Oh, what a delightful surprise!" Mrs. Finklestein exclaimed, her wrinkled face breaking into a warm smile.

Merry stepped forward, presenting a tin of cookies. "Merry Christmas, Mrs. Finklestein! We thought you might enjoy some of our special holiday treats."

As Mrs. Finklestein accepted the tin, Klaus added with a gentle bow, "We hope they bring you as much joy as your beautiful knitted scarves bring to the town."

Mrs. Finklestein's eyes misted over. "You two are angels, truly. Come in for a moment, won't you?"

Inside, they chatted briefly about the town's festive decorations and Mrs. Finklestein's plans for the day. As they were leaving, the old woman pulled Merry into a tight hug.

"You've brought such light to our little town, dear," she whispered.

Merry felt a lump form in her throat. "Thank you," she managed, squeezing Mrs. Finklestein's hand.

Back in the car, Merry turned to Klaus, her eyes shining. "Did you see how happy she was? It's moments like these that make everything worthwhile."

Klaus nodded, his eyes twinkling with centuries of wisdom. "Indeed. The true spirit of Christmas lives in these small acts of kindness."

As they continued their rounds, Merry couldn't help but notice the way Klaus's presence seemed to enchant everyone they met. Children's eyes widened in wonder, and adults found themselves sharing long-forgotten Christmas memories.

"You have quite the effect on people," Merry observed as they left the Johnsons' house, where Mr. Johnson had regaled them with tales of his childhood Christmases.

Klaus smiled enigmatically. "Perhaps they simply sense the magic of the season. After all, isn't that what you've been spreading all along with your grandmother's recipes?"

Merry laughed, a sound as clear and bright as sleigh bells. "I suppose you're right. We make quite the team, don't we?"

As they drove to their next stop, Merry's heart felt fuller than she ever thought possible. This Christmas in Tannenbaum Falls was turning out to be more magical than she could have ever imagined.

The last rays of sunlight painted the sky in hues of orange and pink as Merry and Klaus stepped through their front door. Warmth enveloped them, a stark contrast to the crisp winter air outside. Merry sighed contentedly, slipping off her coat and boots.

"What a day," she breathed, her green eyes sparkling with joy. "I don't think I've ever felt so... fulfilled on Christmas."

Klaus nodded, his dark eyes reflecting the twinkling lights of their Christmas tree. "It was truly special," he agreed, his voice soft and rich with emotion.

They made their way to the couch, sinking into its plush cushions. Merry instinctively curled into Klaus's side, and he wrapped an arm around her, pulling her close.

"You know," Merry began, tracing patterns on Klaus's sweater, "I never imagined I'd find this kind of happiness when I first came to Tannenbaum Falls. It felt like such a big change, taking over Grandma's bakery."

Klaus chuckled softly, the sound rumbling in his chest. "Life has a way of surprising us, doesn't it? Even after centuries, I find myself amazed by the twists and turns of fate."

Merry lifted her head, meeting his gaze. "I'm so glad fate brought us together," she whispered, her heart swelling with affection.

"As am I, my dear," Klaus replied, gently brushing a strand of auburn hair from her face. "You've brought a light to my life I didn't know I was missing."

They sat in comfortable silence for a moment, basking in each other's presence. Merry's mind wandered to the day's events, recalling the joy on people's faces as they delivered cookies and spread cheer.

"Klaus," she said suddenly, "do you think we made a difference today? Really made people's Christmas brighter?"

Klaus smiled, his eyes crinkling at the corners. "Without a doubt. The magic of Christmas isn't in grand gestures, but in the small moments of connection and kindness. Today, we created countless such moments."

Merry snuggled closer, feeling a profound sense of peace wash over her. "You're right," she murmured. "It's been the perfect Christmas."

As the room grew darker, illuminated only by the soft glow of the Christmas lights, Merry and Klaus remained cuddled together, savoring the quiet moments and reflecting on the beautiful day they'd shared with their families and community. In that moment, surrounded by love and warmth, Merry knew she had found her true home in Tannenbaum Falls.

# A Very Krampus Christmas

## Spiced Gingerbread Cookies with a Fiery Kick

These gingerbread cookies have all the warm, classic flavors you love—molasses, cinnamon, and ginger—but with a secret ingredient that takes them to another level: **a touch of cayenne pepper**! The subtle heat lingers just enough to complement the rich spices, making these cookies a standout at any holiday gathering.

### Ingredients

**Dry Ingredients:**

- 3 cups all-purpose flour
- 1 tablespoon ground ginger
- 2 teaspoons ground cinnamon
- ½ teaspoon ground cloves
- ½ teaspoon ground nutmeg
- ½ teaspoon cayenne pepper (*the secret spicy kick!*)
- ½ teaspoon salt
- 1 teaspoon baking soda

**Wet Ingredients:**

- ¾ cup unsalted butter, softened
- ¾ cup packed dark brown sugar
- 1 large egg
- ½ cup unsulphured molasses
- 1 teaspoon vanilla extract

### Instructions

1. **Prepare the Dough:**
    - In a medium bowl, whisk together the flour, ginger, cinnamon, cloves, nutmeg, cayenne, salt, and baking soda.

- In a large mixing bowl, beat the softened butter and brown sugar until light and fluffy (about 2 minutes).
- Add the egg, molasses, and vanilla, mixing until well combined.
- Gradually add the dry ingredients to the wet ingredients, mixing on low speed until a dough forms.

2. **Chill the Dough:**

- Divide the dough into two discs, wrap in plastic wrap, and refrigerate for at least 2 hours (or up to overnight).

3. **Roll and Cut:**

- Preheat oven to 350°F (175°C) and line baking sheets with parchment paper.
- Lightly flour a surface and roll out the dough to about ¼-inch thickness.
- Use cookie cutters to cut out shapes and place them on the prepared baking sheets.

4. **Bake:**

- Bake for **8-10 minutes** until the edges are set but the centers remain slightly soft.
- Let cookies cool on the baking sheet for 5 minutes before transferring to a wire rack to cool completely.

5. **Decorate (Optional):**

- Once cooled, decorate with royal icing or dust with powdered sugar for a festive touch.

**Notes:**

- If you want a stronger spicy kick, increase the cayenne pepper to **¾ teaspoon**.
- These cookies store well in an airtight container for up to **one week** or can be frozen for up to **three months**.

## Cinnamon-Spiced Snickerdoodles with a Twist

This snickerdoodle recipe stays true to the soft, chewy, and cinnamon-coated classic, but with an extra layer of warmth: **a touch of cardamom and brown butter**. The brown butter deepens the richness, while cardamom subtly enhances the cinnamon-sugar coating, making these cookies extra cozy and flavorful.

### Ingredients

#### For the Cookie Dough:

- 2 ¾ cups all-purpose flour
- 1 teaspoon cream of tartar
- 1 teaspoon baking soda
- ½ teaspoon salt
- ½ teaspoon ground cinnamon
- ½ teaspoon ground cardamom (*optional, but adds a warm twist!*)
- 1 cup unsalted butter, browned and cooled slightly
- 1 ¼ cups granulated sugar
- ¼ cup packed light brown sugar
- 2 large eggs
- 2 teaspoons vanilla extract

#### For the Cinnamon-Sugar Coating:

- ¼ cup granulated sugar
- 1 tablespoon ground cinnamon

### Instructions

1. **Brown the Butter:**
    - In a saucepan over medium heat, melt the butter. Stir continuously until it turns golden brown and smells nutty. Remove from heat and let cool slightly before using.

2. **Make the Dough:**
   - In a medium bowl, whisk together the flour, cream of tartar, baking soda, salt, cinnamon, and cardamom.
   - In a large mixing bowl, combine the browned butter, granulated sugar, and brown sugar. Beat until smooth and slightly fluffy.
   - Add the eggs one at a time, mixing well after each. Stir in the vanilla extract.
   - Gradually add the dry ingredients, mixing just until combined.
3. **Chill the Dough:**
   - Cover and refrigerate the dough for at least 30 minutes (or up to overnight for deeper flavor).
4. **Prepare the Coating & Shape the Cookies:**
   - Preheat oven to **350°F (175°C)** and line baking sheets with parchment paper.
   - Mix the granulated sugar and cinnamon in a small bowl.
   - Roll dough into 1 ½-inch balls, then roll each in the cinnamon-sugar mixture. Place them about 2 inches apart on the baking sheet.
5. **Bake:**
   - Bake for **9-11 minutes** until the edges are set but the centers still look soft. The cookies will continue to bake slightly as they cool.
   - Let cool on the baking sheet for 5 minutes before transferring to a wire rack.

**Storage & Notes:**
- Store in an airtight container for up to **5 days** at room temperature or freeze for up to **3 months**.
- For an extra-soft texture, underbake slightly and let the residual heat finish the job.

- The browned butter adds a nutty richness, making these even more addictive!

## Buttery Wedding Cookies with Toasted Nuts

These melt-in-your-mouth **Wedding Cookies** (also known as Mexican Wedding Cookies or Russian Tea Cakes) have a rich, buttery base with toasted nuts for extra depth of flavor. A double coating of powdered sugar gives them their signature snowy look, making them perfect for weddings, holidays, or any special occasion.

### Ingredients

**For the Cookies:**

- 1 cup unsalted butter, softened
- ½ cup powdered sugar
- 1 teaspoon vanilla extract
- 2 cups all-purpose flour
- ¼ teaspoon salt
- 1 cup toasted nuts, finely chopped (*walnuts, pecans, or almonds work well!*)

**For the Coating:**

- 1 ½ cups powdered sugar

### Instructions

1. **Toast the Nuts:**
    - Preheat oven to **350°F (175°C)**.
    - Spread the chopped nuts on a baking sheet and toast for **5-7 minutes**, until fragrant. Let them cool before mixing into the dough.
2. **Make the Dough:**
    - In a large bowl, beat the softened butter and powdered sugar until creamy and smooth (about 2 minutes).

- Mix in the vanilla extract.
- In a separate bowl, whisk together the flour and salt.
- Gradually add the dry ingredients to the butter mixture, stirring until combined.
- Fold in the toasted nuts. The dough will be crumbly but should hold together when pressed.

3. **Chill the Dough:**

- Cover and refrigerate for **30 minutes** to firm up the dough.

4. **Shape and Bake:**

- Preheat oven to **350°F (175°C)** and line a baking sheet with parchment paper.
- Roll the dough into **1-inch balls** and place them about **1 inch apart** on the baking sheet.
- Bake for **12-14 minutes**, or until the bottoms are lightly golden but the tops remain pale.

5. **Coat in Powdered Sugar:**

- Let the cookies cool for **5 minutes**, then roll them in powdered sugar while still warm.
- Let them cool completely, then roll them again in powdered sugar for a perfect, snowy finish.

**Storage & Notes:**

- Store in an airtight container for up to **1 week** at room temperature.
- For extra flavor, add ½ **teaspoon almond extract** or a pinch of cinnamon to the dough.
- These cookies freeze beautifully—just coat them in a fresh layer of powdered sugar after thawing.

## Indoor Decorations

### 1. DIY Paper Garlands & Banners

- Make **paper snowflakes, autumn leaves, or heart garlands** using colored construction paper or old book pages.
- String them across doorways, mantels, or stair railings.
- Cut out **letters to spell festive messages** like "Welcome" or "Home Sweet Home."

### 2. Twinkle Light Magic

- Drape **string lights** over bookshelves, mirrors, and mantels.
- Fill mason jars or glass vases with fairy lights for a cozy glow.
- Wrap lights around a curtain rod for a **starry window effect.**

### 3. Repurpose Old Jars & Bottles

- Use **glass jars** as candle holders or vases.
- Fill bottles with twigs, dried flowers, or fairy lights.
- Paint old wine bottles with metallic paint for a **chic modern look.**

### 4. Cozy Pillow & Blanket Swap

- **Switch out pillowcases** with seasonal covers (or make your own using fabric scraps).
- Layer blankets on sofas and chairs to make the space **extra inviting.**
- DIY **no-sew pillow covers** using scarves or thrifted sweaters.

### 5. Nature-Inspired Decor

- Collect **pinecones, acorns, and branches** from outside for a rustic centerpiece.
- Use dried orange slices, cinnamon sticks, or herbs to make scented décor.

- Arrange **small potted plants or greenery** in recycled containers.

## 6. Washi Tape Wall Art & Frames

- Use colorful **washi tape** to create geometric designs on walls.
- Outline doors or picture frames with washi tape for a **funky, modern touch.**
- Make your own **photo wall** by taping up pictures in creative shapes (like a heart or tree).

## 7. DIY Chalkboard or Whiteboard

- Paint a section of a wall or an old picture frame with **chalkboard paint** for notes, quotes, and doodles.
- Use a cheap whiteboard for a **seasonal message board** near the entryway.

---

# Outdoor Decorations

## 8. DIY Lanterns & Luminaries

- Place **mason jars with candles** along your walkway.
- Use **paper bags with tea lights** to create magical luminaries.
- Fill clear plastic bottles with fairy lights for **DIY outdoor lanterns.**

## 9. Upcycled Wreaths & Door Hangers

- Make a **wreath** from old fabric scraps, newspaper, or even coffee filters.
- Use **twigs and twine** to create a rustic door hanger.
- Hang a picture frame on your door with **seasonal decorations inside** (leaves, flowers, or mini ornaments).

## 10. DIY Painted Rocks

- Collect smooth rocks and **paint them with fun messages** or designs.
- Use them to **line your walkway** or place them in flower beds.
- Write **kindness messages** and leave them in the neighborhood for others to find.

## 11. Hanging DIY Decor

- Make **wind chimes** from old silverware, keys, or seashells.
- Hang **empty picture frames** on a fence or tree for an artsy touch.
- Use an old ladder as a **vertical plant stand** for potted flowers.

## 12. Upcycled Planters & Garden Decor

- Turn old boots, tin cans, or teacups into **quirky plant pots**.
- Use an old **wooden crate as a planter** for herbs or flowers.
- Stack wooden pallets for an **outdoor bench or garden shelf**.

## 13. Sidewalk Chalk Fun

- Draw **fun designs or welcome messages** on your driveway or porch.
- Create a **DIY hopscotch or tic-tac-toe board** for kids (or adults!).

## 14. String Light Canopy

- Hang **string lights over your patio** or along fences.
- Wrap **tree trunks or bushes** with white or colored fairy lights.
- Use **solar-powered lanterns** to keep things glowing at night.

## 15. Repurpose Christmas Lights Year-Round

- Drape them around a **front porch railing** for a magical glow.
- Use them inside **clear plastic or glass bottles** for DIY lanterns.
- String them in **trees or bushes** for an enchanted garden feel.

## Bonus Budget-Friendly Tips!

✔ **Thrift Stores & Dollar Stores** – Find frames, vases, fabric, and seasonal decorations for cheap!
✔ **Reuse & Repurpose** – Old furniture, scrap fabric, and leftover holiday decorations can be refreshed with paint or glue.
✔ **Nature is Free!** – Collect leaves, twigs, shells, and stones for creative decorations.
✔ **DIY Everything!** – Make it a fun project with friends or family!

## DIY Wreaths: Easy & Affordable Instructions

Making your own wreath is **fun, customizable, and budget-friendly**! You can create one for **any season or holiday** using simple materials like twigs, fabric, or even upcycled household items. Below are different DIY **wreath ideas** with step-by-step instructions.

---

# 1. Classic Natural Twig Wreath

**Perfect for: Rustic, farmhouse, or nature-inspired decor**

## Materials:

✔ A bundle of thin, flexible branches (willow, grapevine, or any bendable twigs)
✔ Floral wire or twine
✔ Hot glue gun (optional for decorations)
✔ Dried flowers, pinecones, or greenery (optional)

## Instructions:

1. **Shape the Base** – Gather a few long twigs and bend them into a circle. Overlap the ends and secure them with floral wire or twine.
2. **Build Thickness** – Keep adding more twigs, weaving them around the original circle to create a **full, sturdy shape**. Secure with wire as needed.
3. **Decorate (Optional)** – Hot glue dried flowers, pinecones, or small sprigs of greenery around the wreath.
4. **Hang It** – Use twine, ribbon, or a metal hook to hang your wreath on the door.

## 2. Fabric Scraps or Ribbon Wreath

🧵 **Perfect for:** Upcycling old fabric, holiday themes, and colorful door decor

### Materials:

✔ Wire wreath frame (or make your own using a wire hanger bent into a circle)
✔ Fabric scraps, ribbon, or burlap
✔ Scissors

### Instructions:

1. **Cut Fabric or Ribbon** – Cut your fabric into strips (about **1-2 inches wide and 8 inches long**).
2. **Tie Onto the Frame** – Simply knot the fabric strips around the frame. Keep tying them close together to **create a full, fluffy wreath**.
3. **Mix & Match** – Use different patterns or colors for a **layered, festive effect**.
4. **Fluff & Hang** – Once full, fluff up the fabric pieces and trim if needed. Hang with a ribbon!

---

## 3. Upcycled Pool Noodle or Foam Wreath

🏠 **Perfect for:** Lightweight, large wreaths for any occasion

### Materials:

✔ Pool noodle or foam tubing
✔ Duct tape
✔ Fabric, burlap, or twine for wrapping
✔ Hot glue gun
✔ Artificial flowers, ornaments, or other embellishments

## Instructions:

1. **Form the Base** – Bend the pool noodle into a circle and secure the ends together with duct tape.
2. **Wrap the Base** – Cover the noodle with burlap, twine, or fabric strips. Glue or tuck the ends in place.
3. **Decorate** – Attach faux flowers, mini pumpkins, ornaments, or bows with hot glue.
4. **Hang & Enjoy** – Use a ribbon or hook to hang your wreath!

---

# 4. DIY Grapevine Wreath

🍂 **Perfect for: Seasonal wreaths (fall, Christmas, spring)**

## Materials:

✔ Pre-made grapevine wreath (or DIY one using vines/twigs)
✔ Faux or dried flowers
✔ Greenery (eucalyptus, ivy, pine branches)
✔ Floral wire & hot glue gun
✔ Seasonal decorations (mini pumpkins, berries, pinecones, ornaments, etc.)

## Instructions:

1. **Choose Your Theme** – Decide on a **color scheme or seasonal vibe** (e.g., fall = warm oranges, Christmas = red & green).
2. **Attach Greenery First** – Use floral wire to secure greenery around the wreath base. Keep the flow in one direction.
3. **Add Flowers or Accents** – Arrange flowers, ornaments, or small decorations and secure them with hot glue.
4. **Finish & Hang** – Add a bow or ribbon at the top and hang on your front door!

# 5. DIY Coffee Filter or Paper Wreath

♣ **Perfect for: Budget-friendly, farmhouse chic, or minimalist decor**

## Materials:

✔ Cardboard or foam wreath base
✔ White coffee filters or tissue paper
✔ Hot glue gun
✔ Ribbon for hanging

## Instructions:

1. **Make the Base** – Cut out a large ring from sturdy cardboard (about **12 inches wide**).
2. **Shape the Coffee Filters** – Crumple or fluff each coffee filter into a **flower-like shape**.
3. **Glue to the Base** – Hot glue each coffee filter onto the base, layering them closely for a **full, fluffy effect**.
4. **Decorate (Optional)** – Add faux flowers, glitter, or spray paint for color.
5. **Hang & Admire** – Attach a ribbon or loop for hanging!

---

## Bonus Ideas!

✔ 🎃 **Halloween Wreath:** Use black mesh, plastic spiders, and orange ribbon.
✔ ❄ **Winter Wreath:** Add pinecones, silver spray paint, and faux snow.
✔ 🌸 **Spring Wreath:** Decorate with pastel flowers and butterflies.
✔ 💝 **Valentine's Wreath:** Use pink and red ribbons or cut-out hearts.

### DIY Sock Snowmen – No-Sew Craft 🧦

These **adorable sock snowmen** are easy to make, budget-friendly, and perfect for decorating or gifting! No sewing required—just some socks, rice, and a little creativity!

---

### 🧦 Materials Needed:

- ✔ **1 white sock** (for the body)
- ✔ **1 colorful sock** (for the hat & scarf)
- ✔ **1 cup uncooked rice or polyfill** (for stuffing)
- ✔ **3 small rubber bands** or twine
- ✔ **Hot glue gun or fabric glue**
- ✔ **Buttons, pom-poms, beads, or fabric scraps** (for decoration)
- ✔ **Black and orange markers or felt** (for the eyes and carrot nose)
- ✔ **Ribbon or twine** (optional for a scarf)

---

### 🛠 Instructions:

**Step 1: Create the Snowman Body**

1. **Fill the White Sock** – Pour **about 1 cup of rice** (or polyfill) into the bottom of the white sock. This will make the base of the snowman.
2. **Shape the Body** – Tie a rubber band **tightly above the rice** to create the snowman's base.
3. **Add the Head** – Pour more rice into the sock **above the first section** (about ½ cup), then tie another rubber band to form the head.

### Step 2: Dress the Snowman

1. **Make the Hat** – Cut the toe section off the colorful sock and roll it up like a beanie. Slip it onto the snowman's head. Secure with glue if needed.
2. **Add a Scarf** – Use the remaining part of the sock (or a ribbon/twine) to tie around the snowman's neck as a scarf.

---

### Step 3: Add the Face & Details

1. **Eyes & Nose** –
   - Draw two **black dots** for the eyes with a marker.
   - For the nose, draw a **tiny orange triangle**, or glue on a small felt/carrot-shaped piece.
2. **Buttons** – Glue on **small buttons or pom-poms** down the snowman's belly.
3. **Optional: Arms** – Use **small twigs or pipe cleaners** for stick arms and tuck them into the sock.

---

### ❄ Extra Ideas:

✔ Use **glitter glue or puff paint** for a sparkly snowman.
✔ Make a **family of snowmen** in different sizes!
✔ Give them **tiny accessories** like mini earmuffs (cotton balls + pipe cleaners).
✔ Fill them with scented rice (add a drop of cinnamon or peppermint essential oil) for **fragrant holiday decor**!

---

### 🎄 How to Display Them?

- Place them on a **mantel or entryway table** for a wintery touch.
- Use them as **adorable centerpieces** for holiday dinners.
- Gift them as **homemade Christmas presents**!

## DIY Dollar Store Jar Snow Globes ❄

These **easy, budget-friendly snow globes** are perfect for holiday decorating or gifting! Using simple materials from the dollar store, you can create a magical winter wonderland in a jar.

---

## 🛒 Materials Needed:

- ✔ **Clear glass or plastic jar** (Mason jars or any food jars work great!)
- ✔ **Small holiday figurines** (mini trees, snowmen, reindeer, etc.)
- ✔ **Glitter or fake snow** (white, silver, or iridescent for a snowy effect)
- ✔ **Glycerin or clear glue** (to slow the glitter movement)
- ✔ **Distilled water** (prevents cloudiness over time)
- ✔ **Waterproof strong glue or hot glue gun**
- ✔ **Ribbon, twine, or washi tape** (for decoration)

---

## 🛠 Instructions:

**Step 1: Prepare the Jar & Figurines**

1. **Clean & Dry the Jar** – Make sure your jar is completely clean and dry.
2. **Glue the Figurine** –
    - Use **waterproof glue** to attach the figurine to the **inside of the jar lid**.
    - Let it dry completely (about **1-2 hours** for strong glue, or 10 minutes for hot glue).

## Step 2: Add the Snowy Effect

1. **Fill the Jar** – Pour **distilled water** into the jar, leaving about **½ inch of space** at the top.
2. **Add Glycerin or Clear Glue** – Add **½ to 1 teaspoon of glycerin or clear glue** to make the glitter fall slowly like real snow.
3. **Sprinkle in Glitter or Fake Snow** – Add a pinch of glitter or **tiny Styrofoam snowflakes** for a magical snowfall effect.

---

## Step 3: Seal the Snow Globe

1. **Tightly Screw the Lid On** – Once your figurine is dry, screw the lid back onto the jar **upside down** so the figurine is inside the water.
2. **Seal It** – Apply a **thin layer of waterproof glue around the rim** before closing to prevent leaks. Let it dry for a few hours.

---

## Step 4: Decorate & Shake!

1. **Add a Ribbon or Twine** – Wrap a **festive ribbon** around the lid for extra charm.
2. **Personalize It** – Add a **tag, stickers, or write a holiday message** on the jar.
3. **Shake & Enjoy!** – Flip it over and watch your winter wonderland come to life!

---

## ❄ Fun Variations:

✔ **Mini Santa's Workshop** – Use mini toy gifts, elves, or Santa figurines.
✔ **Winter Wonderland** – Add **tiny houses, deer, or bottlebrush trees** for a cozy village.
✔ **Themed Snow Globe** – Use favorite **cartoon characters, dinosaurs, or superheroes** for kids!

## A Very Krampus Christmas

✔ **Glowing Globe** – Use **LED fairy lights** inside for a magical night glow.

##  DIY Clothespin Stockings
*(Perfect for hanging mini treats or holiday decor!)*

### 🛒 Materials Needed:

✔ Wooden **clothespins** (regular or jumbo size)
✔ Hot glue gun or craft glue
✔ Fabric scraps, felt, or old socks
✔ Paint, markers, or washi tape (optional for decorating)
✔ Ribbon, string, or twine
✔ Small holiday embellishments (buttons, tiny bows, bells)

---

### 🛠 Instructions:

**Step 1: Prepare the Clothespins**

1. **Disassemble the Clothespins** – Carefully remove the metal spring so you have two wooden pieces.
2. **Glue Together** – Lay two flat clothespin halves side by side (smooth sides up) and glue the edges together to form a **stocking shape**.
3. **Let Dry Completely** before moving to the next step.

---

### Step 2: Decorate the Stocking

1. **Paint or Stain the Wood** – Use red, white, or green paint for a festive look. Let it dry.
2. **Add Fabric for a Cozy Look** –
   - Cut out a small stocking shape from felt or fabric and glue it over the clothespins.
   - Add a mini **white felt cuff** at the top for a classic stocking look.

---

### Step 3: Add a Hanger & Embellishments

1. **Glue a Ribbon or Twine Loop** to the back so you can hang it on a mantle or tree.
2. **Decorate** – Add mini bows, jingle bells, or tiny name tags for personalization!
3. **Fill with Mini Treats** – Slip in a candy cane, tiny note, or ornament inside for extra charm.

✨ **Optional Idea:** Use **mini clothespins** and hang them on twine to create a **DIY stocking garland**!

---

## 🎄 DIY Popsicle Stick Christmas Tree Ornaments

(*Easy, fun, and great for kids!*)

### 🛒 Materials Needed:

✔ **Popsicle sticks** (regular or jumbo size)
✔ Green, red, or gold paint
✔ Hot glue gun or craft glue
✔ Small pom-poms, sequins, beads, buttons (for ornaments)
✔ Twine or ribbon (for hanging)

## 🛠 Instructions:

### Step 1: Build the Christmas Tree Shape

1. **Arrange 3 Popsicle Sticks** into a triangle shape for a **tree base**. Glue the ends together and let dry.
2. **Add a Popsicle Stick Trunk** – Cut a small piece from another stick and glue it to the bottom of the triangle.

### Step 2: Paint & Decorate

1. **Paint the Tree** – Use **green paint** for the triangle and **brown for the trunk**. Let it dry.
2. **Add Ornaments** – Glue on small **pom-poms, buttons, sequins, or beads** to decorate like Christmas baubles.
3. **Top it Off** – Add a **tiny star, ribbon bow, or jingle bell** at the top.

### Step 3: Add a Hanger & Display

1. **Glue a Ribbon or Twine Loop** to the back.
2. **Let Dry & Hang on Your Christmas Tree!** 🎄

✨ **Bonus Ideas:**

✔ **Rustic Look** – Leave the popsicle sticks unpainted and use natural twine.

✔ **Snowy Effect** – Dab **white paint or glitter glue** on the edges for a snowy finish.

✔ **Photo Frame Tree** – Glue a tiny **photo of a loved one** inside the triangle as a keepsake ornament.

## DIY Easy-Sew Family Pajamas Using Fleece or Flannel 🧵👪

Making **cozy, matching pajamas** for the whole family is easier than you think! With **fleece or flannel**, you can create **soft, warm pajama pants and shirts** using a simple **DIY pattern from existing clothes**. This tutorial focuses on pajama pants (the easiest to sew), but you can also make matching tops by following the same method.

## 🛒 Materials Needed:

- ✔ **Fleece or flannel fabric** (2-3 yards per adult, 1-2 yards per child)
- ✔ **Elastic (1-inch wide)** for the waistband
- ✔ **Matching thread**
- ✔ **Fabric scissors or rotary cutter**
- ✔ **Sewing machine (or hand-sewing needle)**
- ✔ **Pins or fabric clips**
- ✔ **Measuring tape**
- ✔ **Iron (optional for crisp seams)**

## Step 1: Make Your DIY Pattern

1 **Choose an Old Pair of Pajama Pants** – Find a pair that fits well (for each family member).
2 **Fold the Pants in Half** – Lay them on **butcher paper, newspaper, or wrapping paper** to trace a pattern.
3 **Trace Around the Pants** – Add **1 inch extra for seam allowance** all around and **2 inches at the top** for the waistband.

4 **Cut Out the Pattern** – This will be your **DIY pajama pants template**!

♦ *For kids' sizes,* use their existing PJs and follow the same steps.

---

## Step 2: Cut the Fabric

[1] **Fold the Fabric** – Place your fabric **double-layered** so you get two identical pieces for each pant leg.
[2] **Lay Your Pattern on Top** – Pin it down and **cut around the pattern**.
[3] **Repeat for All Sizes** – Cut enough fabric for **each family member's pants**.

---

## Step 3: Sew the Pajama Pants

[1] **Sew the Inner Leg Seams**

- Place **two fabric pieces right sides together**.
- Sew along the **inner leg seam** on both pant legs using a **straight stitch**, then reinforce with a **zigzag stitch** to prevent fraying.

[2] **Sew the Crotch Seam**

- Turn **one pant leg inside out** and place the other leg inside it (so they're right sides facing each other).
- Line up the **crotch seams** and sew across.

[3] **Make the Waistband**

- Fold down the **top edge by 1 inch**, then fold again by another **1 inch** to create a casing for the elastic.
- Sew along the edge, leaving **a 2-inch opening** to insert the elastic.

[4] **Insert the Elastic**

- Cut a piece of **elastic about 1-2 inches smaller than the waist measurement**.
- Attach a **safety pin** to one end and **feed it through the waistband casing**.
- Sew the **elastic ends together**, then close the opening with a straight stitch.

5 **Hem the Bottoms**

- Fold the **bottom edges of the pant legs up ½ inch**, then fold again another **½ inch** and sew for a clean hem.

## 🎄 Step 4: Optional Matching Pajama Tops

To make **simple matching tops**, use a **loose-fitting T-shirt** to create a DIY pattern, follow the same cutting method, and sew the sides and sleeves together. You can even **add fun cuffs or a contrast fabric pocket** for extra style!

## 🎄 Fun Variations & Personalization

✔ **Add Pockets** – Cut two **small squares** of fabric and sew them onto the front.
✔ **Make a Jogger Style** – Add **cuffed ankles** by sewing a band of stretchy fabric at the bottom.
✔ **Monogram or Appliqué** – Use **iron-on letters** or sew a **fun holiday shape** (snowflake, reindeer) on the leg.
✔ **Use Drawstring Instead of Elastic** – Leave an opening in the waistband for a ribbon or shoelace tie.

A Very Krampus Christmas

## Final Touch: Match the Whole Family!
🎅 Make **Christmas pajamas** with holiday prints
👶 Sew a **mini version for toddlers & pets**
💝 Use **different color cuffs** for each person

✨ **And there you have it—cozy, homemade family pajamas in just a few easy steps!** Let me know if you want **a tutorial for matching nightgowns or pajama tops** too! ☺

Patti Petrone Miller

Praise For Author "Patti Petrone Miller's books hit different from your typical feel-good stories. Sure, Hallmark's got their formula down pat, but Miller brings something fresh to the table - authentic characters that actually feel like people you know, dealing with real-life stuff while still keeping things wonderfully uplifting.
I honestly get the same warm fuzzies reading her books as I do curling up with hot cocoa for a Hallmark marathon, but without all the predictable plot points we've seen a million times. She's nailed that sweet spot between heartwarming and genuine that's super hard to find these days. If you're looking for stories that'll leave you smiling but don't make you roll your eyes at how perfect everything is, Miller's your girl. She's got that special touch that makes you feel like you're hanging out with friends rather than just reading about characters. Move over, Hallmark - there's a new queen of wholesome in town!"

## ABOUT THE AUTHOR

Ladies and gentlemen, step right up to "Where the Magic Happens" - a literary circus that'll make your bookshelf do backflips!

Meet Patti, the ringmaster of this wordy wonderland! She's not just an Executive Producer; she's a word-wrangling wizard, conjuring up an animated TV series based on "ELLIOT FINDS A HOME." It's the tail-wagging tale of a thumbs-up pup and his silent sidekick, proving that you don't need words when you've got opposable digits and a heart of gold!

Hold onto your bestseller lists, folks! This Polygon Entertainment superstar has hit the USA TODAY jackpot and Amazon's #1 spot more times than a cat has lives. With 7 dozen books under her belt, she's got more genres than a chameleon has colors. From Urban Fantasy to Horror, she's been spinning yarns longer than your grandma's knitting needles!

But wait, there's more! Patti's life is like a celebrity bingo card:

She rocked "Romper Room" at 4, probably making the other kids look like amateur rompers.

She rubbed elbows with Captain Kangaroo and Mr. Green Jeans. (No word on whether the jeans were actually green.)

She shared a train ride and a sandwich with Sidney Poitier. Talk about a meal ticket to stardom!

## Patti Petrone Miller

She high-fived President Nixon at the circus. Who knew the circus could get any more political?

She went to school with David Copperfield. We assume she didn't disappear during attendance.

She roller-skated with pre-famous John Travolta. Grease lightning, indeed!

She sipped cocoa with Abe Vigoda. Fish never tasted so sweet!

When she's not busy being a literary legend, Patti's juggling roles faster than a circus performer. Teacher, grandma, furparent - she does it all with a smile that could light up a haunted house.

When she's not busy being a literary legend, Patti's juggling roles faster than a circus performer. Teacher, grandma, furparent - she does it all with a smile that could light up a haunted house.

Speaking of haunted houses, meet the "Queen of Halloween" herself! This Wiccan High Priestess is stirring up stories spookier than a skeleton's dance moves. Her books are flying off the shelves faster than witches on broomsticks, so follow her on social media or risk missing out on the hocus-pocus!

So, come one, come all, to Patti's phantasmagorical world of words! It's more exciting than a roller coaster, more magical than a rabbit in a hat, and more diverse than a box of assorted chocolates. Don't be shy - step into the spotlight and join the literary party where the pages turn themselves and the stories never end!

# A Very Krampus Christmas

www.ingramcontent.com/pod-product-compliance
Lightning Source LLC
LaVergne TN
LVHW041814060526
838201LV00046B/1262